CROSSING THE RED LINE

S.L. STERLING

CROSSING THE RED LINE

by

S.L. Sterling

Crossing the Red Line

Copyright © 2025 by S.L. Sterling

ISBN: 978-1-998649-02-0

Paperback ISBN: 978-1-998649-03-7

Editor: Brandi Aquino, Editing Done Write

Cover Design: Thunderstruck Cover Design

Ella Larson is allergic to me.

I don't blame her; we do have a history, and I can be what you could call uncooperative at times. So, it's not a wonder she looks stressed when she comes to tell me I've been selected as the new face of a promotional opportunity for the Dominators.

As we talk, I find out there's another source of her stress, she's also allergic to wedding season, at least that is what she tells me when she finds out her friend is getting married.

I hate to see pretty girls stressed, so I offer to be her date for her friends wedding and to cooperate for the promotional event I've just been assigned to. When she looks at me wondering where the catch is, I drop the bomb. I need something from her. I need her to come with me to visit my mother and be my fake girlfriend for the weekend. A simple exchange, two friends helping on another.

Little did I know how this one little exchange would end up blowing up in both our faces and making us face a reality we both thought didn't exist anymore.

Chapter One

Ella

I KNEW I never should have opened the email, I thought as I stared at my screen. How many more times would I have to learn this lesson the hard way?

I let out a sigh and picked up my mug, bringing it to my lips, irritated that the coffee had gone cold. I let out a sigh and got up out of my chair, heading to the coffeemaker, where I poured more hot coffee into my mug and returned to my desk.

I sat back down and stared at the 'Save the Date' email, my stomach turning. There was no way I'd make it through yet another wedding season, watching more of my friends venture down that doomsday path.

A couple of my friends had been married less than a year and they already had issues, and it seemed none of the single ones learned from the ones before. My best friend was currently dealing with the fact she couldn't get pregnant while another one faced marriage counselling after finding out her husband of eight months was already cheating on her.

I moved the email into my deal-with-it-later folder. If there was one thing I'd learned, it was that I was never getting married, especially after seeing how their lives were unfolding. I turned my focus on only work-related emails. It was the only way I'd be able to move on with my day without either being sick or having a panic attack.

I quickly skimmed down the list and stopped when I saw an email titled *Change to the Children's Hospital Campaign*. I let out a sigh, wondering what could have changed in the last two days that I wasn't aware of, since I was supposed to be the one who oversaw this.

Ella,

Because of the timing of the Dominator's games, and that Lucas Clark has been pulled because of a minor knee injury, both Knox Evans and Dylan Hayes will have to attend away games on the dates of the filming of this campaign. Effective immediately, we have substituted

Lucas in their place. I request you meet with Lucas to bring him up to speed about the charity and about the photo shoot.

Pamela Smith,
Head of Public Relations

Guy Larson,
Owner of the Vancouver Dominators

I SHOULD HAVE JUST RESPONDED to the other email instead; I thought as my stomach flipped. Of all the players on the team, why did it have to be Lucas who'd been assigned to this project? Was this some sort of joke the universe was playing on me?

He was the only player on the team that gave me a hard time about working for my father, his boss, the owner of the Vancouver Dominators. Aurora and Lorelai both said it was because he had a crush on me, but I shoved that comment under the rug almost as fast as I had shoved that email into the folder. Little did they know, Lucas and I had dated once upon a time, and his behaviour had nothing to do with what they thought it did.

I took a moment, trying to center myself. Then I got up from my desk, grabbed the folder containing all the information about the campaign, and made my way out of the office and down to the lunch area.

I made my way through the halls, wondering if I should just turn around and reply to that email instead of walking headfirst into an inferno. However, I knew it had to be done, and I'd rather rip the bandaid off, instead of prolonging the inevitable.

I stopped outside the lunchroom door, taking in a deep, cleansing breath, once again centering myself. On the third deep breath, the scent of chicken parmesan hit my nose, making my stomach growl. I rounded the corner and stepped into the room to see Lucas sitting there, sports section and a plate of food in front of him, ready to dig in.

I let out a sigh and approached the table, folder in hand, avoiding his eyes.

"Well, well, if it isn't Ella." He winked. "What's Guy got you up to today? Spying on us boys, so you can tell Daddy all the horrid things we say in the locker room?" He chuckled.

I frowned. When had Lucas become such an ass? I wondered.

"Look, it wasn't my fault my father caught word of what happened in the locker room the night you grabbed my ass when I first started," I said, staring him right in the eye.

Yep, you heard that. He'd thought I'd been lying when I told him about my new position with the team, and to prove it, he'd pushed me up against the locker room wall, looked me directly in the eyes, kissed me, and grabbed my ass.

That had been my welcome to the team, and when my father caught wind of it, he'd asked me if it had been true. I couldn't stand there and deny it. The mere memory of it had made me blush when he confronted me, so I'd told him the truth. Although we'd dated, and we'd been extremely intimate, Lucas had gotten in shit for the lack of respect he'd shown me. He'd been lucky Daddy took pity on him and hadn't suspended him, but it had started this reaction every time I had to interact with him.

"Sure, whatever you say," he murmured, digging into his food.

"Lucas, despite what you might choose to believe, I never said a word. He asked me, and I don't lie to my father. You know that." I gritted, giving him an evil glare.

"Whoa, tone it down there. If looks could kill, I'd be dead on the spot." He chuckled, shoving another forkful of food into his mouth. "There was a time you'd never have told your father anything that went on between us, the nights in my car out back of the arena, the night I took you in your father's kitchen, the night in the locker room after my very first game with the Dominators. Don't think for one second, I've forgotten any of that."

I stared at him, at that smug smile on his face, and jumped as my cell phone rang. I pulled it from my pocket and glanced at the screen in time to see my best friend's name flash on the screen. Rolling my eyes and turning away from Lucas, I answered the call.

"I can't talk right now," I barked.

"Don't give me that. Why haven't you responded yet?"

I shook my head and looked over my shoulder to see Lucas staring at me with curiosity.

"Well???"

"Layla, I'm at work."

"Yes, but I need to know if you'll be at the wedding."

Irritation flooded me, and I threw the folder on the table and slid into the chair across from Lucas, burying my face into my hands.

"You know I hate weddings."

"But it's my wedding and you are my maid of honour."

I let out a sigh, then quickly glanced at my calendar to see if the date was free. Sure enough, just as I suspected, I had nothing booked for that weekend.

"Fine, I'll respond the moment I return to the office, okay? Now, I've got to go."

I hung up the phone and placed it down on the table with more force than I'd planned. I could feel Lucas staring at me but refused to look at him. I just wanted him to go away. I wanted everyone to go away and leave me alone to sulk in my misery.

"What's got you so down?" he questioned, pulling me out of my inner turmoil.

"Why would you care?"

"Despite what some people in this room think of me, I have a caring side, and I don't like to see pretty girls sad. So, spill it."

I let out a sigh and picked at the corner of the folder I'd brought in, imagining how this was going to sound to not only my ex-boyfriend but to a guy like him. A guy who could get any girl at the drop of a hat.

"Well, I'm waiting?"

"Remember Layla, my best friend from college?"

"Yes."

"She is getting married and wants me to be her maid of honor."

"That is great," he said, holding out his fork with a piece of breaded chicken smothered in sauce and cheese for me to take, but I shook my head.

"It's not great."

"Why isn't it? You should be happy for her. She found the one."

"Yeah, it's great," I muttered.

"It is. Why would you think otherwise?"

"Oh, I don't know. Let's look at it, shall we? Janet has been married a little more than a year and is on the verge of a breakdown because she can't get pregnant. Maxine has been married six months and is already in marriage counselling because she found out that Max is cheating on her. I don't even have a decent boyfriend, actually never have had, and here they are getting ready to settle down, and I'm over here ready to give up on love." I put my head down on the table.

"Never had a decent boyfriend? Geez, thanks. I didn't think I was that bad."

I bit the inside of my cheek to stop myself from saying something I'd probably regret. Lucas was right, he hadn't been horrible, he'd just been so focused on hockey and the idea of us.

Or maybe it was I who went along the wayside.

"All good things come in time," I heard him say.

"Yeah, says the guy who can have whatever girl he wants."

Lucas chuckled. "Ella, you really have a slanted view of us, don't you?"

"It's true. You all have girls throwing themselves at you. Even Dylan and Knox still have women lining up, and they are both going to be tying the knot in the coming months. Clay is just a manwhore…and well, the others on the team are…"

"Just because we have girls throwing themselves at us doesn't mean we take advantage of that. Besides, those women are so shallow, and while they can be fun, we look for the real side of people. To be honest, I can't remember the last time I even went on an actual date."

"Whatever…" I said, rolling my eyes.

"It's the truth. I've been single for so long I actually made up a girlfriend just to get my mother to stop asking me if I were seeing someone, and now all she does is bug me to bring her out to see her?"

"Why would you lie to your mother if you don't remember the last time you dated someone?"

"Because she wouldn't take the truth as an answer. So, I made one up."

"That's ridiculous. What are you going to do when she demands to meet her?"

"I was using work as the reason why I could get home, but now with the knee injury and she knows I'm not playing, she won't take the work excuse much longer either. I'm screwed."

"Lucas, that is horrible. You should be ashamed of yourself, using work as an excuse to not see your own mother."

Lucas gave me a sexy grin. "It's not because I don't want to see her, but because I have no one to take with me. Like I said earlier, I'm painfully single, just like you."

It was then my phone rang again, and when I looked at the screen, I rolled my eyes and let out a huff.

"What?" I said through clenched teeth as I answered the call.

"Will you be bringing anyone?" I heard Layla ask.

"Doubt it. I'd probably have to pay someone to go with me," I barked. "Talk later." I quickly hung up, putting my phone down, meeting Lucas's eyes.

"You know, they say stress is horrible for a person, especially outside stress that is interfering with the workplace."

"Is that so?"

"Yes, which makes me think you could benefit from a vacation," he said.

I frowned. "A vacation?"

"Yeah, you should take some time to talk to your father, see if he can't give you a little time off."

"No, thanks. I'm not sucking up to Daddy because I'm having a hard time."

"Okay then," Lucas said, digging back into his meal. With the fork halfway to his mouth, his eyes lit up, and he looked up at me. "Okay, what if it were a free vacation? On the weekend?"

I studied Lucas's eyes, trying to see where he was going with this, and when he gave me that stupid, sexy, shit-eating grin he normally had, I put it all together.

"You aren't serious?" I questioned.

"Sure am. An all-expenses paid trip out to Vegas for the long weekend. All you need to do is pretend to be my ever-so-loving girlfriend, again, in front of my mother for a few days. It will give you the time you need to sort yourself out, deal with all this stuff you're carrying, and let loose and have some fun. What do you say?"

I looked around the room, wondering if one of the other players had put him up to this.

"What about my father?" I questioned.

"I won't mention it if you won't." Lucas shrugged.

I thought for a moment. The photoshoot for the campaign wasn't for another couple of weeks, and this would give me the time I needed to go over things with him. Plus, he might be right; it might help me unwind and relax if I got out of the city and away from everything.

"You said all expenses paid?" I questioned.

"Yep, everything: flight, food, accommodation, all covered."

"And all I need to do is pretend to be your ever so loving girlfriend? Again?"

"That is all."

"I don't know, Lucas. Won't this be opening up a

can of whoop ass with your mother? I mean, I'm sure she is going to remember me."

"Of course she's going to remember you. She wanted us to get married and have babies, which she still throws in my face every now and again. It will at least quiet her up for a while. Give me the mental break I need from the constant harping of finding someone."

I didn't know if I should agree or not, but I also knew Lucas hated the type of spotlight I was going to be putting him into, and I needed him to do this campaign, so if I were going to do this for him, he had to agree to do this for me.

"I'll do it, but only on two conditions."

Lucas looked over at me. "Two conditions?"

"Yes, two," I said, not faltering at all.

He let out a sigh, dug his fork into his food, and then muttered, "Okay, name it."

Lucas must have been desperate to get his mother off his back. He never succumbed this quickly.

"That you be my date for my friend's wedding this summer?"

"And the other?" he questioned.

"That you take part in this campaign, since I've been told you are replacing Dylan and Knox because you are out on injury," I countered.

Lucas hated doing any type of publicity, which was

why when I saw the email, I knew I'd have my work cut out for me. There was no way I could do another wedding solo, and if he said no, then I'd just curl up in my condo, have a good cry, then put on my big girl panties and deal with not only forcing him to do the campaign, but suffering through the wedding just like I'd done the past two.

At first, he said nothing while he shoved a few bites of food into his mouth. It was as if he were enjoying watching me squirm, which he probably was. After a few minutes, he finally looked over at me.

"Alright, Larson, you got it. Just let me know what I need to do and I'll do it," he said, extending his hand across the table for me to shake.

Chapter Two

Lucas

I'D BEEN SO desperate to appease my mother, I really didn't even realize what I'd agreed to, I thought to myself as we made our way through the airport. What had I been thinking when asking my ex-girlfriend, whom my sisters and mother had loved, to join me this weekend and play the ever-so-doting girlfriend?

Also, whose bright idea was it to decide to travel on a long weekend? I was so used to getting preferential treatment with the team, I'd forgotten how busy airports were on weekends like this. I slipped my ball cap on and forced my way through the crowd while Ella walked slowly behind me.

"I can't believe I let you talk me into this," she said as she struggled to keep up.

I talked her into this. I let out a huff. I didn't talk her into anything. I simply mentioned she looked like she needed some time away.

"Me talk you into this?" I said.

"Yes, you flashed the offer of a free trip when you knew I desperately needed one, and don't say you didn't. We dated long enough for you to know the signs of me being burnt out and stressed."

"Just do me a favor and don't get lost. The last thing I need is to have to go back into that mess of people to find you, increasing my chances of being recognized," I said, finally spotting the fake last name I'd used when I booked the taxi.

"You remember I hate crowds, right?" Ella questioned. "You really think I'm going to just wander off?"

"Look, there's our ride," I said, reaching around and guiding her to the front of me as we made our way toward the driver.

"That isn't our ride," Ella said, stopping. "It says Keller."

I leaned down, bringing my mouth to the edge of her ear. Immediately, all I could smell was the scent of her skin and perfume, a scent I'd loved at one point and, according to my body's response, still did. "That's right, that is the name I gave. Otherwise, we'd face the possibility of being mauled to death if someone recognized me."

"Oh, please." She shrugged her shoulder, her cheeks flushing as I placed my hand on the small of her back, leading her forward. "You aren't that popular."

"Do you want to find out?" I questioned, ready to blow my cover just to prove her wrong.

"Not really."

"That's what I thought."

I nodded toward the driver, and he quickly grabbed our bags, shoving them into the trunk of the cab while we climbed into the back seat.

"Where are we staying?" Ella questioned, checking her email as she sat beside me.

"I got us a two-bedroom suite at the Palazzo. Figured it was better than staying with my mother."

I sat back in the cab and waited for the driver to pull away from the curb and take us over to the hotel.

"Why aren't we staying with your mother?" Ella questioned.

I couldn't help but chuckle. "You don't know what my mother is like now that she's moved out here." I winked.

"I don't have to. It's your mother. I'm sure she is still the loving woman she always was."

"That's right, that is what you remember, but

believe me, she changed, and it is my mother. Trust me, sweetheart, you'll be happier in the suite." I winked.

Ella elbowed me in the side as the cab pulled away, and when I looked down at her, she grinned up at me.

"Lucas, again, you should be ashamed of yourself."

I couldn't help but burst into laughter. "Okay, but you'll see."

Half an hour later, we stepped into the suite at The Palazzo. I watched as Ella walked inside and looked around at the room and then checked out the two bedrooms while I paid the bellhop for delivering our bags. Then I shut the door, leaving the two of us alone.

"Well?" I questioned, slipping my shoes off and heading toward the couch to make myself comfortable after being squished in the plane and in the back of the cab.

"It's amazing!" she said, making her way over to the window and taking in the view. "Can I have that room?" she questioned, pointing at the one on the right. "It has an amazing bathtub, and you know how much I love taking baths."

"You can have it," I said, putting my feet up on the end of the couch and lying down, flipping the TV on to catch the sports news.

"Thanks," she said, running her hand along the mini bar. "Want a drink?"

"Sure, I'll have water," I said.

"Water? You aren't playing this weekend?"

"Nope, but I'm also not drinking. I have tests that need to be completed when I get back so I can get my knee looked at, and if I need any type of surgery, I'll heal faster if I look after myself."

I glanced over at Ella, who was bent over, looking in the little fridge. She still had that perfect round ass, one that I'd never been able to keep my hands off. I wished I didn't need to now, I thought as I quickly adjusted myself before she turned around.

"Have whatever you want. Don't let me stop you," I said.

"Really? You sure?"

"I'm sure, cupcake," I said. "No need to worry about the cost, either. Take whatever your heart desires."

Within a couple of minutes, Ella held a bottle of water out to me and then sat down on the table in front of me with her glass of wine.

"So, I think we need to sort out a few details, don't you?" she questioned, taking a drink.

"About?" I was paying more attention to what was being said about me on the news regarding my injury than to her.

"About us?"

I looked over at her, noting the serious look on her face.

"It's easy. We reconnected at work. Found out that our breakup was a mistake, and quickly found out that we couldn't keep our hands off one another." I shrugged.

"I'm not telling your mother that!" Ella screeched.

I couldn't help but laugh as her face turned red. "Why not?"

"Why not?" she repeated.

"Yes, why not? Is there something wrong with me?" I questioned.

"No!"

"Well, then?"

Ella let out a sigh. "Lucas, I'm not telling your mother I couldn't leave her son alone. So, you better figure something else out."

"It's not like she wouldn't believe it. We used to be that way with one another, in case you've forgotten."

Ella shook her head. "Trust me, I haven't forgotten. I also haven't forgotten how much more you cared for the game than for me. If only I'd been a hockey stick, we'd probably have little mini stick children by now," she gritted.

"You're ridiculous."

"I am not. I'm stating a fact."

"Fine, you're stating a fact." I huffed, annoyed by

her insistence I was the issue with our previous relationship ending. "Why don't you tell me what we should tell my mother, then? Let's see if you have a better idea?"

Ella shook her head and took a sip of her wine. "Never mind, Lucas. We'll use your story."

"No way. Come on, share with me some ideas. I'm sure we can find something in one of them we can use. It would help if you filled me in on what and who you've been doing since we split."

"Pardon?" she gritted, her eyes narrowing at me.

I chuckled. "What's wrong? Got a bit of a shady past since we ended?"

"No," she said, becoming defensive.

"Well then, why not tell your boyfriend all about it?" I said, reaching out and grabbing her side, causing her to laugh.

"Stop." She pushed my hand away so she wouldn't spill her wine. "What time are we meeting your mom for dinner?"

"Six-thirty, we are meeting at a restaurant just downstairs."

I watched as she glanced at her watch and then nodded, looking around. "I think I'm going to take a hot bath, get ready for dinner."

I watched as she got up and made her way around the end of the table, watching her take that gorgeous body away from me. Once she was just about to the door, I cleared my throat.

"Ella?"

"Yeah?" She turned and looked over at me.

"Can I watch?"

She did nothing but shake her head.

"Can't blame me for trying." I chuckled.

When she turned away from me, I was certain I caught what might have been a small smile on her lips.

Chapter Three

Ella

I CLIMBED out of the hot water and wrapped myself in one of the large plush towels, then grabbed another and wrapped it around my head. I felt a million times better and way more relaxed after that bath—and the rest of my glass of wine.

I glanced at myself in the mirror, taking in the worry on my face. What was I worried about? Perhaps it would have helped me to have more of a backstory. Maybe what was really bothering me was the fact I had jumped into this with my eyes closed, like I had done with everything in my life since Lucas and I had ended.

That was probably why I was still single. I'd made

one poor decision after the next in my love life and personal life. For some strange reason, when Lucas suggested this idea, I didn't want to let him down. I knew exactly what this sort of pressure from family felt like. My father was the same, always throwing in his two cents about the fact all my friends were getting married, and then there was me.

I let out a sigh; I felt almost sick with nerves. I inhaled deeply, taking in the powerful scent of the lavender oil I'd used in my tub, exhaling slowly, trying to calm myself a little. I guess if Lucas was okay with things the way they were, then I should just relax and go with the flow.

I squeezed some moisturizer into my hands and was about to rub it on my legs when my phone pinged. I opened up my messages to see that Aurora had posted in our group chat with Lorelai. They'd welcomed me into their group with open arms after one of the Dominators' functions at the beginning of the season.

While I was hesitant at first to befriend anyone who worked with the team because of who my father was and, of course, my past with Lucas, the girls were persistent. Once I learned Lorelai was the little sister to Phil, and that both the girls were dating two of the players on the team, Dylan Hayes and Knox Evans, I decided it might not be so bad.

I hadn't told them about my past with Lucas, mainly because I didn't want to hear that I should give him a second chance. I'd heard that enough from my other friends. Lately, I'd heard it from my father as well, which had shocked me after he'd been so angry from the initial incident.

As I read the message, I realized that this weekend the three of us had planned on shopping, dinner, and then going to the movies since the team was on a set of away games.

I knew Aurora had been looking forward to getting out. Her morning sickness had been so bad she'd basically been bedridden, and since she had finally started feeling better, she had been looking forward to dinner out at The Lighthouse.

I let out a sigh. I really had messed this up, hadn't I. I'd snuck off without so much as a word to anyone, and now I would have no choice but to explain to them where I was—and with who.

Quickly, I hit respond and explained I was feeling under the weather, wondering if we could plan to go on Monday instead. Almost immediately, they both understood, agreed to the date change, and wished me well.

"You just about ready?" I heard Lucas question outside the bathroom door.

I glanced at myself in the bathroom mirror. "Give

me half an hour."

I heard him mutter something about this being one reason we'd ended and why he wasn't in a relationship as he walked away. I just rolled my eyes.

Twenty minutes later, my hair dried and styled, I slipped into the green dress I'd brought for tonight and then took a moment to look at myself in the mirror, smoothing out the material. Then I slipped my feet into the black heels I'd brought, grabbed my clutch, and took off toward the common area of the suite.

Lucas lay on the couch watching the hockey game, wearing dress pants and a shirt, and just as I entered, he shouted at the TV as he glanced quickly in my direction. He was about to look back at the TV, but stopped and took a second look at me, his eyes skimming my body.

"Holy shit, Larson, you clean up pretty good," he said, sitting up and shutting the TV off, his eyes still glued to me.

"Thank you, but you know that already. I figured I'd better look good. After all, it is the first time seeing your mother again after we've gotten back together." I winked.

Lucas chuckled as he stood up and grabbed the key card off the table, shoving it into his suit jacket.

"Alright, I'm glad to see you are on board with everything."

"I'm just trying to have fun and get in the game."

"Great. It will make it more believable that way." He grabbed my ass as he went to open the door, causing me to jump.

Lucas broke out in laughter as I turned and glared at him. Then he shrugged his shoulders and winked at me. "Remember, believable, and if you were mine again, my hands would be glued to you every chance I got."

"Too bad they weren't the first time," I said, feeling my cheeks heat at his comment.

"Not going to let my want to follow my dreams go, are you?" he asked.

"Want to follow your dream? Please, you were going to the NHL regardless, and you knew it. You just made me feel second place is all, but I'm over it. Now, let's go meet your mother."

Neither of us said a word to one another in the elevator. Lucas stood there looking forward, and I stood there feeling awful about what I'd said. We had both been to blame for our breakup. I had no reason to be a bitch to him, yet I hadn't been able to help myself.

When we stepped off the elevator, each of us looked in the opposite direction to find the restaurant. There was nothing but stores in the direction I was looking, and when I went to tell Lucas that, I felt him take my hand in his.

"This way."

We made our way through the restaurant, Lucas leading the way. Finally, he paused and glanced over his shoulder at me.

"You ready?"

I smiled, hoping this wasn't a huge mistake, and nodded as he pulled me up beside him. There in front of us sat his mother and sisters, all of them staring at us in shock.

"Mom, you remember Ella," Lucas said, his hand resting on the small of my back. "Ella, you remember my mother, Dorothy, and my sisters, Janice and Corinne?" He nodded toward the two girls who sat there looking dumbfounded.

"Ella, it's wonderful to see you, darling," Lucas's mother said, taking hold of my hand and then pulling me in for a hug.

"You as well," I said, feeling my body tense as she hugged me.

His mother had barely let me go when I faced his first sister, Janice. She gave me a questioning look as she, too, gave me a hug, welcoming me. When she let go, Corinne stepped in front of me. She looked me up and down and then placed her hands on her hips and turned toward Lucas.

"Ella Larson? Your ex-girlfriend from your college

days? Guy Larson's daughter?" She pursed her lips, looking at me.

Alarm bells went off inside me as she turned toward her brother. Corinne had never really liked me, but she acted as if I were a different person just because her brother now played for the team my father owned.

"What?" his mother said, turning back toward us.

I could feel my heart beating so hard I felt as if I were going to faint. Lucas didn't falter, instead he wrapped his arm around my waist, which I was thankful for, and cleared his throat.

"I know what you all must be thinking. Yes, this is Guy Larson's daughter. I am dating my boss's daughter, but remember, I have dated her before," he said proudly. "Which, to be honest, is why we have kept it so hush-hush. We had to, you know, to keep it out of the media."

Thank god he'd come up with that because I was just about to blurt out everything to relieve the stress I was feeling.

"Do you really think this is a good idea, Lucas?" Corrine asked. "Things have changed. Ella was once just Ella. Now you are dipping your stick in the—"

"Do you think I care? I can't help who I fall in love with," he blurted, cutting her off.

"It's your career. You should fucking care. You

worked hard to get to where you are and have been with the Dominators for your entire career. I don't think the owner would be happy to know you are scre—"

"Whoa, Corinne, that is enough," Lucas's mother said, stepping in. "Ella, darling, why don't you come and sit with me?" she said, guiding me over to an empty chair, while Lucas slipped into the one beside mine.

Lucas's mother asked us some questions while we looked over the menu and finally placed an order. I answered each question but could still feel Corinne staring at me with questioning eyes.

The moment the table quieted, she looked at her brother and I and cleared her throat. "So, what do the guys on the team think about you doing the owner's daughter? That must cause some tension in the locker room," she said, resting her chin on her palm.

"Not really. That is why we've kept it so hush-hush," Lucas said.

It was then I placed my hand on his forearm. "Yes, it was my idea, to be honest. I see how Lucas is with his teammates, and I really didn't want any tension between them. As for my father, he approved of Lucas when I was younger. I can't imagine his thoughts would have changed over the years. Remember, he isn't only Lucas's boss but mine as well, and my father cares more about the team than anything. A player like Lucas is an asset. We haven't told my father we are back together yet and probably won't until the end of the season. I don't want to disrupt the team's winning streak either."

"Is that because you care more about your father than my brother?" Corrine asked, tapping her fingers on the table.

"Not at all. Lucas cares about the team and the playoffs, and he has asked me if it's okay for us to wait to share about our coming back together. Since it's important to him, I want to respect his wishes."

"Oh, please," Corinne mumbled, rolling her eyes.

"Corinne, that is enough," Dorothy barked. "Ella, that shows me you care about my son very much. When my daughters started dating their significant others, they both wanted the entire world to know. There was no keeping them quiet about it. I can see you aren't the same as my daughters. I really admire that you will keep the news about your relationship with Lucas quiet, even though I'm sure in the hockey circles it's an enormous deal. You want to let other women know he's taken. However, the fact that you care more about him and his love for the game and his relationships with his teammates than sharing the news that you two are together tells me you are one special girl, and I hope my Lucas knows that."

"Of course I know that, Mom," Lucas chimed in.

I turned to him, gently smiled, and was about to say something to his mother when the servers arrived with our food. Within minutes, everyone was eating, and wine had been poured. I worked hard to reconnect with his sisters, and shortly after dessert had been served, Janice and even Corinne came around and started sharing pictures of their kids with me.

I don't know how it happened but before long, I had agreed to an invitation to spend Christmas and New Year's with Lucas and his family.

I was having such a good time that it made me sad when Lucas tapped me on the shoulder and leaned into me, letting me know the time. I glanced down at my watch to see it was almost nine thirty.

"You're dragging her away?" Corinne questioned, looking up at her brother.

"I am. It's not too often we get to spend the nights together, if you catch my drift." He winked.

"Ugh, please, I don't want to know anything about your sex life," Janice said, holding up her hand, causing me and Corinne to laugh.

"That's good, because I wasn't sharing," he answered.

"Okay, so we will see you guys at Christmas then," Janice and Corinne said at the same time.

I smiled and nodded, but out of the corner of my

eye, I caught the look on Lucas's face. In my heart I felt bad, because I knew this was all fake, and I had always really liked his sisters and his mother.

"Actually, we should get together tomorrow and do some shopping," Corinne said, looking at her mother and sister.

"That is a great idea," Lucas's mom said, looking at the pair of us.

I looked up at Lucas and waited for his lead before I agreed to go. He paused for a moment, almost like a deer in headlights. I was certain he had figured tonight would be fine and then tomorrow we would just go back to being Lucas and Ella. He nodded and then smiled down at me.

"Lucas, you better be there tomorrow," Janice said, standing up to give her brother a hug.

I watched as Lucas hugged Janice, then Corinne, and then his mother. It warmed my heart knowing he had such a caring family, something I wished I had. My father had always supported me, but if my mother had stuck around, perhaps he wouldn't have become so bitter.

"Ella, darling, I'm happy to see you are back in Lucas's life. He missed you, and I know you are the right choice for him, even if he didn't see it the first time," Dorothy said, pulling me in for another hug.

Chapter Four

Lucas

"SHE'S A GEM, darling. Don't let her go this time," my mother whispered as she hugged me one more time.

I'd been proud of how well Ella coped in such an awkward situation. She'd surpassed all of my expectations. Like before, she hit it off with my mother and she'd shown that we were 'the real deal.' She also smoothed things over with Corinne, which wasn't ever an easy feat.

In fact, she'd sold the idea of us so well with each brief touch, brief whisper, and smile that I even had to reel myself in throughout the night. I was so grateful to her for helping me with this and selling the entire relationship idea, I wasn't even sure I knew if what she'd asked me to do would be enough to repay her.

We stepped out of the restaurant and began walking toward the elevator we'd come down in when I stopped and turned to her.

"Are you tired?" I questioned.

Ella smiled at me and shook her head. "Not in the slightest."

"Feel like going out for a couple of drinks?"

She glanced around at the people walking past us and then shrugged her shoulders. "Not sure. I've never been to Vegas."

"What? You've never been to Vegas? Guy Larson's only daughter has never been to Vegas?" I questioned.

She laughed. Maybe my surprise sounded silly to her, but this was *Vegas* we were talking about. How had she never been?

"Nope, never." She shrugged.

I grinned. "Well, you are definitely in Vegas with the right Dominator. I love it here."

"Why does it sound like I should be afraid of that?" she asked, giggling.

"Not a thing to be afraid of. Let's go," I said, taking her hand in mine and pulling her toward the exit door of the hotel.

We headed to a quiet little place the boys and I had found one of the last times we'd come to Vegas for a game, and the pair of us snuck inside. We grabbed a table near the back of the bar and ordered a few drinks.

"I can't believe you've never been here," I said again as I passed her the drink I'd ordered for her.

"What's this?" she questioned.

"Just trust me," I said, waiting while she stared at the drink.

"Oh god, I don't think so." Ella giggled.

"Come on, just trust me. I would let nothing happen to you," I assured her, handing her the drink.

She cautiously accepted it and took a sip. Her eyes lit up as she smiled. "Oh, that is yummy."

"I told you. Stick with me, babe, I won't steer you wrong."

"Keep feeding me these drinks and you don't have to worry about me going anywhere," she said, sucking down more of the drink.

"Whoa, Ella, slow down. Those are strong. You'll be on your face if you don't."

She looked up at me with those gorgeous brown eyes and smiled. "Would you catch me?"

I couldn't do anything but shake my head as she placed her empty glass down on the table. Those drinks had been a disaster for Dylan the first time he'd had them right after he'd broken up with Carlie. It had taken him almost three days to recover. There was no way I could allow her to have any more.

"Would you like another drink?" I heard someone ask, and I looked over to the edge of the table to see the server standing there and Ella shaking her glass.

"I think we are gonna pass on another one of those," I said, catching the nasty look Ella was giving me for cutting her off before she'd gotten started. "Perhaps just a gin and tonic for her."

"I don't want a gin and tonic. I want another one of those," she told the server, completely ignoring what I'd said.

If she wanted a hangover from hell, who the hell was I to stop it? The server glanced at me, and I simply nodded and watched as she walked away. When I turned back to Ella, she sat there watching me strangely.

"Why don't you want me to have another one of those?" she questioned.

"It's not that I don't want you to. I just don't want to see you in pain tomorrow for shopping with my sisters and mother, remember? Those drinks, they have a kick to them, best enjoyed one per night. Just ask Hayes." I chuckled, remembering how much of a damn baby he'd been the next day.

"Oh, I sense a story," she said, clapping her hands together. "You know I love a story."

"Oh, there is one, but it's best to ask him. I wouldn't want to ruin his opportunity to relive that night." I chuckled.

"Do you guys like to torture each other?"

"Damn straight. Don't bet for a single second that if I did something stupid they wouldn't be all over me to relive it. The worst part is, they'd make shit up to go with it if given the opportunity."

"That's horrible."

"Nah, not horrible. Its just guys being guys." I winked. "Can't take it personally. I know in a heartbeat I could go to any one of them if I needed something, and they'd be there."

"Wow, so almost like brothers."

"You got it. Which, as you know, I wasn't lucky enough to have."

"Yeah, but it seems like your sisters still really care about you."

I nodded. "But you saw how they reacted tonight at first."

"Yeah, but I think that was because they'd caught onto your game of avoidance and figured you were lying about being with someone. Either that or they were just shocked to see me there with you."

"Well, I need to thank you for being such a good sport. You really helped make it believable."

"Not a problem. It was fun. I just don't know what we are going to do about Christmas and New Year's now." She laughed as she took a sip of the fresh drink the server had placed on the table.

She met my eyes as the music got louder.

"Want to dance?" I questioned, nodding toward the dance floor.

"Sure." She shrugged, placing her drink down and sliding out from her seat.

We laughed and danced to the next four songs before the music changed to a slow song. As she smiled at me and went to leave the dance floor, I reached out and grabbed the back of her sweater, pulling her back toward me.

Things were easier with Ella than they'd ever been. In fact, all night it felt as if we'd never broken up, and that was only because everything felt so fucking easy.

"What?" She smiled as she turned around and faced me.

"Dance with me?" I asked, my voice low.

She studied my eyes and her expression grew serious. I wrapped my arms around her waist, pulling her close to me. The beat of the music and the gentle swaying of our bodies made it difficult for me to take my eyes off her. I pulled her tighter, and with her hands shaking, she slowly slipped her arms around my neck and looked up at me.

I couldn't stop myself. I wet my lips and brought my mouth to hers, kissing her hard. I expected a slap when I pulled away, but when she didn't fight me, I wrapped my hand in her hair and brought my lips back to hers, my tongue washing through her mouth.

The moment the song was over, I pulled her off the dance floor. I wanted to be hidden behind the door of our room, in private, where things could go further should we want them to.

"Where are we going?" she asked as I dropped some money on the table and led her out of the bar.

"Back to the hotel," I said.

It wasn't long before we entered the Palazzo and headed to the elevators. The moment we were back inside our room, I took her and pressed her up against the wall, kissing her hard.

It had been hard enough not to take her downstairs right outside the bar, but now, in the privacy of our own suite, I wasn't holding back. I wanted her.

I kissed her lips, down the side of her neck to her shoulders. She ran her fingers through my thick hair and let out a tiny moan when I brought my lips back to hers. I reached around her as I continued to kiss her and pulled at the zipper at the back of her dress. Slowly inching it down, I pulled the material off her shoulders, letting her dress fall to a pile at her feet. Our lips parted and my eyes danced down her body, at her full breasts that were spilling out over her bra, to her waist and hips. She was fucking gorgeous.

I could feel my cock hardening at the thought of being inside her, and I grabbed her and hoisted her over my shoulder. She let out a tiny scream followed by a laugh as her hands rested on my ass, balancing herself.

"Don't get too grabby," I said, gently smacking her.

"You either." She giggled as I carried her through the suite and to my bedroom, where I carefully placed her on the floor.

The moment I straightened up, she looked at me, biting her bottom lip as she stepped forward and started undoing the buttons on my shirt one by one until it hung open, exposing my chest. She ran her hands over my abs and up to my pecks, then she looked up at me as she slowly ran her hands back down my chest until I felt her tug at my belt.

"What do you think you're doing?" I questioned, trying hard to keep my breathing steady as she undid my belt, the button on my pants and then my zipper. My pants fell to my feet, and I watched her expression as her eyes washed over me. They were as hungry with need as I'm sure mine were, and as she ran her hand over my boxers, gripping my hardened cock, I couldn't help but inhale deeply.

"Well?" I asked again.

She looked up at me with those hungry eyes. Immediately, I bent down and met her lips again, this time pulling her over toward the bed where we both lay down. I undid her bra with one hand and waited while she slid the straps down her arms, exposing her breasts to me.

I took hold of her hips and guided her to straddle me, then I took her breasts in my hands, feeling the weight of them as I ran my thumbs over her nipples. She closed her eyes and bit her bottom lip as I sat up and took one nipple into my mouth, running my tongue around it, and gently taking it between my teeth.

She wrapped her arms around my head as I continued to suck and flick her nipple with my tongue, and she let out a sexy moan that sent a surge of heat through my body.

When I let her go, she met my lips, kissing me hard. I lifted her off me and moved her onto the bed beside me, my hands exploring her body. I took hold of the waistband of her panties, inching them down her body as I removed my boxers, freeing my aching cock.

"Tell me you brought protection?" she whispered between kisses.

I nodded. I didn't want her to think I'd been hoping this would happen, but you never damn well know, and I'd learned over the years it was always better to be prepared than to be caught in a situation like this without it.

I leaned over, opened the drawer beside the bed and pulled out a condom, holding it out for her, and then lay back against the bed, placing my arms behind my head once she'd taken the condom from me.

I watched her as her eyes fell to my cock, then she carefully ripped open the wrapper. I closed my eyes at the feel of her hand as she rolled the condom on me. She looked up at me, want in her eyes. I didn't waste a second. I pushed her down onto the bed, got up on my knees, careful not to put too much of my weight on my bad knee, and took hold of her legs, pulling her down toward me. She let out a giggle as I lifted her legs up, resting them on my shoulders.

"Ready?" I questioned.

Her eyes gleaming with anticipation, she let out a nervous giggle, then nodded as I lined myself up to her entrance. She was so damn tight, she felt amazing as I began inching my way inside her. I watched her expression and stopped at the first sight of any pain or discomfort. I knew I was larger than most men, and while we'd been together before, I knew it would take her time to adjust to me again.

I met her lips and slid my hand between her legs, my fingers dancing over her clit, hoping to help her relax.

"Lucas…" she moaned as I continued. "You should stop before I…"

"No way, baby, I won't push you over the edge, not yet," I said, watching her as she closed her eyes and fisted the sheets.

When she began breathing faster, I stopped rubbing her, lined myself up at her entrance, and slowly inched my way inside her, stopping to allow her to adjust to me before I slid deeper into her. I went back to drawing slow circles over her clit while pushing myself into her as far as I could go; she let out a deep moan, her fingers digging into my back.

I grabbed one pillow, placed it under her hips, and let her legs fall off my shoulders to rest on my forearms. I leaned forward, meeting her lips as I started thrusting in and out of her. The more she moaned, I quickened my pace, sinking deep into her, and when she shouted my name, something inside me knew I didn't want to let her go. I wanted to claim her, ruin her for anyone else.

I sped up my pace, reached down between us, and stroked her clit as I continued to pound into her. I wanted her to come undone, to remember exactly what it felt like to be with me. I could feel her tighten around me as she screamed my name and dug her nails into my back.

The sound of her moans soon turned to whimpers as I continued to claim her. Before long, I could feel the build of my release at the base of my spine and knew I couldn't hold off. Three more deep pumps were all it took for me to let go.

Chapter Five

Ella

I WAS SO warm and cozy; I didn't want to move, but my head was pounding. I needed some headache tablets badly, so I slowly opened my eyes. My vision was blurry.

I wiped my eyes, the dark room becoming clearer. I lay there staring at the wall, wondering where my suitcase had gone. I was certain I'd left it on this side of the bed. I blinked, rubbing my eyes again, it was too early to worry about it. I just needed those tablets.

I pushed myself up off the mattress, the room spinning out of control, and I lay back down and closed my eyes. That was when I felt the bed move and something touch my leg, and then I heard a man snoring. I swallowed hard as I carefully lifted my head from the pillow and looked to my right.

"What the hell?" I muttered to myself, panic filling me and pain shooting through my temples.

Lucas lay there, sound asleep beside me, his hand on his bare stomach. As I stared at him, all I could think about was last night and what I'd been thinking. I was only here to do the guy a favour; to convince his family he had a girlfriend. I certainly wasn't here to get back together with him.

Careful not to wake him, I rolled over, and that was when I felt the ache in my body. A very unfamiliar, yet familiar, ache, one I hadn't felt in a long time. Five years, to be exact.

I lifted the covers and slipped out from under them, throwing on the first thing I saw before I slipped from the room as quietly as I could. I made my way across the common area and into my room, where I immediately flopped down on the bed and buried my face in my hands.

I wasn't supposed to sleep with him. What the hell was I doing?

It had taken me two years to get over him. The tears I'd shed then had almost bled me dry. I could hear my father now, giving me the responsibility lecture, again. In fact, I could hear him say more things than that, especially since he'd made it so incredibly clear that I wasn't supposed to get involved with any of his players. While I was certain he hadn't included Lucas in that bunch, I didn't want to find out either.

I knew that rule had only been for me, otherwise Aurora and Lorelai might not be working for the Dominators. While Daddy had mentioned Lucas and I dating again recently, I knew he'd hated seeing me hurting during our breakup and had threatened to kill him on more than one occasion. As a matter of fact, it surprised me he hadn't immediately traded Lucas when he took over the Dominators, especially when I started working for him.

I got up off the bed, determined that this could be fixed with a quick conversation and a promise to him and myself not to cross that fine line again. I went into the bathroom, turned on the shower, and then climbed in under the hot spray, washing away the events of last night—and hopefully the ache in my body—but it did little good.

When I finally stepped out of the shower, the only thoughts on my mind were from last night. Where his hands had touched and probed my body. Where and how he'd kissed me, and how many times I'd screamed his name while my legs had been wrapped around his back, arms, and very last, his head.

I dried my hair with my towel and then looked at myself in the mirror. My cheeks and chest were pink the more I thought of last night. Without thinking hard, I could still feel him inside of me, how he'd taken his time, how he'd stretched and filled me so full it actually hurt but felt so good at the same time. I hadn't wanted it to end.

I dropped the towel to the floor and grabbed the shirt I'd had on before I'd gotten in the shower. As I looked at myself in the mirror, I realized it was one of his shirts I'd grabbed by mistake. I took a moment, bringing the material up to my nose, and closed my eyes as I inhaled the scent of him, remembering how it felt to be held in his arms.

"Stop it, Ella," I murmured to myself. "Don't you dare travel back down that trail of memories. It will only provide you with a world of hurt."

I ran into the bedroom, quickly stripped the shirt off me, and got dressed in my own clothes, before heading back into the bathroom to dry and style my hair and put on my makeup. The moment I finished, I tiptoed out into the common area and threw his shirt down on the back of the couch. I then made my way into the small kitchen area and stopped dead in my tracks.

Lucas stood in the kitchen, his back to me, wearing nothing but a pair of boxers. Immediately, my eyes went from his wide shoulders, muscular back, down to his perfect ass, then back up to the mop of messy curls I'd loved running my fingers through last night.

I let out a sigh as my eyes ran down his body once again, noticing his muscles flexing in his forearms as he lifted the coffeepot—

"Are you going to say something, or just stand there?"

I jumped at the sound of his voice, my eyes instantly falling to the floor in case he spun around and caught me looking at him.

"Morning," I squeaked.

"Left me high and dry this morning. What the hell was that? Just a wham bam thank you Lucas? You know, in case you forgot, I enjoy morning-after cuddling just like you do." He turned around, placing a mug of coffee down on the small island in the center of the kitchen and pushing it toward me.

Instantly, my mouth went dry. I hadn't bolted for any other reason other than shock. I leaned forward and picked up the mug of coffee, blew on it before taking a mouthful, hoping that some sort of words came to my mind.

"Ella, you should know that I enjoyed last night, and I'm having an absolute blast with you. It's like old times, and there are absolutely zero regrets over here about what happened between us last night."

My heart skipped a beat as I continued looking at the floor, unsure what the hell to say to that. I enjoyed myself last night as well. There wasn't a doubt in my mind that he already knew that. I didn't need to tell him that, did I.

"Honestly, Ella, I've been thinking of us a lot since you started with the team. There have been so many times I thought about calling you, or coming to your office and talk to you, just to see where you stood with the idea of us, if you were maybe open to trying again, but after your father lost his shit with me over the locker room incident, and you wouldn't even look my way, I decided I wouldn't pursue you. I didn't want it to put any type of pressure on you, and I didn't want any bad blood in the workplace, so I just shoved that idea aside."

Whoa, what the hell? He'd thought about us. He'd thought about maybe one day trying again. I almost wanted to pinch myself to see if this was some sort of dream, because things like this never happened to me. They happened to my best friends, and pretty much everyone around me, but never to me.

"Lucas...I, um...I don't know what to say. I...."

"You don't need to say anything. I don't want there to be any pressure between us. I just figured you should know the truth. I don't want you walking away from this weekend thinking that what happened between us was a mistake…"

"I wasn't sure what it was," I muttered.

Lucas was quiet. I stood there, afraid to look up for fear he was joking around. I wasn't sure I could take it if he was. This was the most shocking and sweetest thing he'd ever done.

"Ella, you can look at me, you know."

With my mug in my hands, I slowly raised my eyes to his. One look at his face told me he was serious. As I looked at him, I wondered if perhaps this time we could have something real. Not that what we had wasn't real before, but maybe now that we were both older, maybe he's ready for more.

"We should get ready to meet your sisters," I said, my voice shaking, wanting to take the focus off what we were talking about, because at this point, I wasn't sure if I should open up on how I was feeling or just shove it back down inside of me.

Lucas pushed himself off the counter. "Yep, you're right, we should. Give me ten," he mumbled, and he took off toward his room, his head down, leaving me in the kitchen alone.

Just like every decision up to this point, I feared I was making another mistake. Why was I so afraid to share how I felt?

Chapter Six

Lucas

I'D WATCHED her most of the day with my sisters. They'd laughed and talked and for a quick moment it felt as if we'd never parted. It warmed my heart to know that she was just as dedicated to helping me after I'd spilled my guts to her this morning as she had been yesterday.

"So, Ella, what's your father like?" my mother asked her while we were eating lunch.

"Mom, you know her father. You've met him before," I said.

"In passing, Lucas. Only in passing."

It was the truth. Her father had been dealing with

many personal issues when Ella and I had dated before, and he was rarely available to deal with anything she needed. When we'd asked him to meet my mother over dinner, he'd done nothing but bark and murmur that all he had time for was to say hello in the driveway.

"It's okay, Lucas," Ella said, placing her hand on mine and squeezing. "It's been a while since they met in passing." She winked before turning back to my mother.

"Well, my father, as you know, now owns the Dominators, so he is pretty business-oriented, more so than ever before. He is also very focused on hockey. He is strict, but very caring for me, and as you know, I don't know my mother biological mother. She left us when I was young. The one thing I've missed about your family is how tight-knit it is. Since Lucas and I split, I wished I had that, as it was something I loved about being with him and with your family when I was younger," Ella added, her eyes watering.

I couldn't help but look at her. It upset me to hear this information. I hadn't realized how much my family and I had meant to her when we dated before. Honestly, I knew I loved her, but I didn't figure we were that serious with one another, and apparently that was because, as she put it, I was too involved with my hockey stick to notice. Now all I could think about was changing this for her, and if she were mine, I'd do just that.

"Well, Ella, you have that now. Don't forget it either. You are part of this family, regardless of what happens between you and my son. You understand that?" my mother said, rubbing the back of her hand.

"I do."

As my mind reeled with this new information, I began feeling a little guilty. Okay, a lot guilty. What I had planned to do after Ella agreed was come here, prove to my mother and sisters that I had a girlfriend, and in a few months break the news that we'd gone our separate ways.

As I sat there, listening to my mother talk about holiday plans, I knew I couldn't just follow the plan I had. Besides, after our time together last night, Ella somehow owned my heart again, and I wondered if she always did. I'd never felt this way about a woman before.

Fuck, I really needed my boys. Both Dylan and Knox had been through this shit. As close as I was to Clay, there was no way I could get any advice from him. Ella was right, he was a manwhore, but he'd been acting so strange lately and had been keeping to himself.

"Will you excuse me for a minute?" I said, placing my knife and fork beside my plate.

Ella looked over at me, concern in her eyes. "Feeling okay?" she asked.

"Yep, just need to take a minute and respond to the coach," I said, pointing to my phone.

"Okay." She turned back to my mother and sisters, getting back to their conversation.

I made my way out of the restaurant and, once outside, I pulled my phone from my pocket and sent off a message to both Dylan and Knox.

Lucas: Got a second? Need some help here.

Dylan: What could you need help with? You are on medical.

Knox: What he said.

I ROLLED MY EYES. These two probably didn't want to be bothered. They'd both just returned home from a string of away games and were more than likely pleasuring their women.

Lucas: I have a situation. I brought a friend to trick my mother and sisters into believing I was in a relationship.

Dylan: Oh, for the love of...

Knox: Say no more Hayes, this sounds like it might be a disaster.

Lucas: It's not a disaster. Well, not yet, but it's turning into one.

Knox: What did you do, bring an ex? HAHAHA

Dylan: That could be the only reason I see it being a disaster as well, Knox. We all know that Clark doesn't have any women friends.

Lucas: Can we be serious for a moment?

I SWALLOWED hard as I stared at the screen. Was I that predictable?

Dylan: Okay, sorry, why is it a disaster?

Lucas: My mother and sisters have invited her for the holidays.

Knox: Your fake girlfriend?

Lucas: Yes.

Dylan: Oh god, I couldn't even have imagined how this might have blown up in your face.

Knox: Same. Lorelai wants to know who the lucky girl is.

Lucas: Why are you telling Lorelai?

Dylan: Aurora wants to know as well.

I ROLLED MY EYES. Why I thought I could count on these two to help was beyond me.

Knox: Don't want to tell us? Want us to guess?

Dylan: Oh, we could have fun with this. Maybe we should bring the girls into the conversation.

Lucas: Don't you dare.

Knox: Inviting now…

Lucas: Knox, if you value our friendship, you won't do it.

Knox: You aren't any fun.

Dylan: Alright, so you take her to Christmas to appease your mother. What's the issue?

Knox: Not a bad idea, Hayes. I mean, right now I don't see any other way out of the problem either. He'd look more like an ass if he broke the girl's heart before Christmas than he would if he did it after.

Dylan: While I disagree, he's going to look like an ass either way, I figure after would be the better choice.

Lucas: I wasn't really coming to you for a solution to that problem.

Dylan: Well then, what are you bothering us for on a Sunday morning? You are well aware of what we reserve our Sunday mornings for.

Knox: Same bro, Lorelai is waiting,
and I hate to keep her waiting.

I SWALLOWED hard as I stared at my phone. I hated interrupting them when they were with their woman, especially since there had been many mornings I'd wished I'd had someone to share my Sunday mornings with. It would be easier if I just told them. Rip the bandaid off.

Lucas: I think I have feelings for her.

Dylan: *almost faints* What? Did I read this right?

Knox: *rubs eyes* yep Hayes, you read it right.

Lucas: Cut the crap. What do I do?

Dylan: Well, are these 'feelings' because of a certain something that might have happened last night or while you've been gone? Or have you just lost your mind?

Knox: ...yeah, did you two fuck?

Dylan: Evans, Lucas is sensitive.

Knox: Precisely why I'm asking...you have to be careful with these sensitive types.

Lucas: Kill it Hayes. See if I ever come to either of you again for advice.

Dylan: Okay, sorry. Seriously, if you like her, then make your move or forever hold your peace.

Knox: Agreed.

Lucas: That's all the pair of you have to say?

Dylan: Damn straight.

Knox: Yep! Make your move!

Lucas: ...and if I don't?

Dylan: If you don't, take her home for the holidays, drag it out even more, and end up way more fucked up afterward.

Knox: Yeah, had I not of taken my chance with Lorelai, it would have ruined me.

Dylan: Yeah, same, and don't tell me you can't. Fuck, I hit on my stepsister. *laughing*

Lucas: Well, all I can say to that is that you are one sick fuck.

Dylan: ...and proud of it. Seriously man, if you like this girl just tell her.

Knox: Speaking of which, who is it?

I COULD FEEL my stomach roll at the thought of telling them who I'd brought. I'd never mentioned a word about Ella before and wasn't sure this was the best way to tell them I'd taken my ex-girlfriend, the owner's daughter, with me.

Lucas: I'll tell you later.

Dylan: Later? WTF?

Knox: Yeah, Lorelai wants to know. She says I am cut off until I tell her, so you better fucking spill it. This man has needs.

Lucas: Got to go. Bye, guys.

Dylan: Chicken shit

Knox: I'm gonna beat your ass against the boards next time I see you if I don't get any, Clark.

Lucas: Tell Lorelai it's not worth torturing you over.

Knox: That's because you don't want an ass whooping. Now, I'm gonna go pin my girl to the mattress if I'm not getting any more answers.

Dylan: Same here…advice hotline is over…

Knox: Sure is.

I SHOVED my phone in my pocket and shook my head and made my way back into the restaurant, where I saw Ella laughing at something my sisters had said. I made my way over to the table and sat back down, Ella immediately turning to me with a smile on her face. She placed her hand on my upper thigh and leaned into me.

"Everything okay?" she questioned.

"All good."

"We'll be right back then," she whispered, placing a soft kiss on my cheek. "We didn't want to leave your mom alone at the table."

I watched as Ella and my sisters made their way across the restaurant and disappeared into the ladies' room. When I turned and faced my mother, she had a serious look on her face.

"What?" I questioned.

"How is everything going between the two of you?" she asked, resting her chin on her hand.

"Well," I said again, my stomach flipping, knowing this was all for show.

"Are you happy?"

I nodded, taking the last mouthful of my food. "I am."

"I really like her, Lucas. I always did. She's good for you."

"I agree," I added, wishing she'd move off this topic. I hated lying to my mother. I picked up my water and took a drink.

"Can we expect to hear wedding bells soon?" she questioned.

I began choking at the question she'd just asked. My mother had been on me since I'd turned thirty-two, wondering when she could expect to have a daughter-in-law. My sisters both had been married since they were in their mid-twenties, one had two kids and the other three. I knew my mother had expected a grandson or granddaughter from me, but I'd put my focus into my career instead.

"Not sure, Mom," I added. "We really haven't talked about it."

It was then Ella and my sisters returned to the table. I'd never been so thankful to see them all, hoping this was the end of the inquisition.

"What haven't we talked about?" Ella asked, sitting down beside me, placing her hand on my upper thigh once again.

"The future," I bit out, hoping she'd hear the agony in my voice and not proceed with any more questions.

"Mom, are you on Lucas about wedding bells again?" Janice questioned, shaking her head.

"Well, I just don't see what it is he is waiting for, if things are going well between the two of them. He should just ask her already."

"Mom!" I exclaimed.

It was then Ella grabbed hold of my hand and resting her hand on my forearm, leaned into me and said, "Yeah, big guy, what are you waiting for?"

I could see the playful look in her eyes and knew she was only saying this to play into the situation, but somewhere inside of me something said not to let her go. I couldn't imagine someone else having her now, especially after last night. Instinctively, I wrapped my arm around her and pulled her into me, pressing a kiss to her cheek.

"What exactly are you hinting at, Ella?" I asked, looking into her eyes while my sisters and mother sat there waiting for her reply.

Chapter Seven

Ella

LUCAS PULLED me close and pressed a kiss to my cheek. It was this sort of moment I missed the most. I closed my eyes and rested my head against his shoulder, which allowed him to place another kiss on my forehead.

"You know, babe, it's not too late for us to rectify this problem of marriage. If you are serious about this, that is." He winked.

At first, my heart jumped into my throat as his blue eyes stared down into mine. Was he serious? I swallowed hard, then my racing heart slowed as I remembered where we were. Vegas, the land of glitz and glamour and fake everything. It would be just like the movies. A silly decision leads you to one of those little chapels on the strip, get married, only to find out the Elvis impersonator who married you was a fake.

Seriously, all those little wedding places weren't real. I knew that because one of Layla's friend had used one to get her ex-boyfriend back by marrying his best friend. He'd flipped out at first only to learn that it was as fake as ever.

"Um…what problem?" I questioned, trying to play into the situation and add a little excitement to everything by pretending I didn't know what he was talking about.

I could feel his mother and sisters watching us, which somehow added extra pressure to the moment. As he studied my eyes, my mind flashed to last night, to the feeling of being with him again. Then I thought of how wonderful this weekend had been, even if we had only been pretending. What a better thing to add to the memory of this weekend but a fake ceremony?

"Don't keep us in suspense. Answer him," I heard his mother say. "I need to know if we should make an appointment for a wedding today."

"Sure, why the hell not?" I said, the words falling from my lips as I stared up into his eyes.

Lucas looked at me, not sure how to respond. Why

did he look shocked? Had he not watched movies? Had I never told him about Layla's friend?

As we stood there staring into one another's eyes, his mother let out a squeal of excitement and began clapping her hands.

"Girls, girls, girls, it looks like there will be a wedding after all!"

I caught Corinne and Janice both whispering something to their mother, but I didn't catch what it was because I hadn't been able to tear my eyes from Lucas. Why did he look so panicked?

I was about to lean over and whisper to Lucas if I could talk to him for a moment and explain to him this wasn't real when I felt someone pull at my hand. As I tore my eyes from Lucas's, I looked down at his mother's phone to see a little chapel on the screen.

"What is this?" I questioned.

"Only the best little chapel in all of Vegas, Midnight Moments. They have an opening in an hour, and I just booked the pair of you in." She smiled, pulling me away from Lucas. "Isn't that wonderful?"

"It looks perfect," I said, feeling giddy inside.

I was about to ask his mother a question when Corinne and Janice took hold of my hand and began leading me away from Lucas and his mother.

"Where are we going?" I questioned.

"Well, you can't marry my bother in jeans and a T-shirt, so we are going to get you a dress."

I looked down at myself. It was a fake wedding chapel; I didn't need to spend any money on a dress, I thought to myself, but didn't want to ruin the moment. The girls continued to pull me toward a shop, and that was when I shrugged and decided I'd just get a dress I could wear again. When I looked up, I saw Lucas and his mother head into a shop for men.

Why were they acting like this was real, I wondered. Regardless, if Lucas was going along with it, who was I to say anything? So instead, I said nothing and began flipping through the dresses on the rack in front of me.

Chapter Eight

Lucas

WE WALKED down the hallway of the hotel toward our room, Ella hanging off my arm. She'd had a lot to drink during our celebratory dinner, and I knew she'd regret it come morning. I also knew the drinking wasn't the only thing she was going to regret come morning, I thought as I guided her down the hall.

I should have been the responsible one. She hated the idea of marriage. She'd told me as much as before we'd left. Yet when she said yes to getting married, some part of me wondered if maybe I could change that for her, which was why instead of being the one to stop it, I went along with it.

Had I been that desperate to have another chance with her? I guess I had, and I knew now that come morning, that second chance would be taken from me the moment she realized exactly what we'd done.

Once we got to our room, I directed her to lean against the wall while I pulled my wallet from my pocket and searched for the key. Finally finding it, I took it and held it against the door and glanced over at Ella to see she was holding her hand out in front of her, frowning as she looked at it.

"Why are you frowning?" I questioned, shoving my foot against the door to keep it from closing on us. "Is something wrong with your hand?"

"You know…" she said, looking over at me, "for a big shot hockey player I thought I'd have gotten a decent sized rock. Instead, my finger is naked." She giggled, holding her hand in my face and hiccupping.

"Forgive me," I mumbled. "I had less than thirty seconds to digest the fact we were getting married, thanks to you and your mouth. Besides, when you sober up in the morning and remember what happened, you'll want out of this quicker than you got into it, and you'll be glad you don't have a rock on that finger, as will I. Trust me."

"Trust you? I did trust you and look at where that got me."

I used my foot to hold the door while I guided her

inside the room before we got into it in the hallway, then shut the door and locked it. Then I bent down, and with one hand on her hip, I grabbed her right shoe, carefully pulling it off her foot, then the left before standing up again and slipping my own shoes off.

"No comment to what I said?" she questioned.

"Where did your trust get you?" I asked, looking down into her face.

She looked up at me, sadness in her eyes.

"Heartbroken, single, hating all men, and wishing now more than ever that I could be lucky enough to have one more chance with you."

I studied the look in her eyes as she looked up at me. Was I really the cause of her unhappiness? That was impossible. We'd broken up a long time ago. There was no way she wasn't over me, was there? Sure, I'd gone down the Ella tunnel occasionally, maybe more often than I should have, but girls didn't do that, did they? They always had guys at their beck and call, more so than us men.

"Not going to say anything to that, are you?" she said, placing her hand on my cheek.

What was I supposed to say? The look in her eyes was enough to kill me. Was I supposed to tell her I was sorry for something I never knew I did?

"It's okay, Lucas. You don't have to say anything. I

am sure it's a lot to learn that your ex-girlfriend still thinks of you and still wants you. If I were sober, I'd never tell you that either," she said, wrapping her arms around me and leaning her head on my chest.

I closed my eyes and wrapped my arms around her. Fuck, she was all I wanted, and truth be told, she was also the reason I'd not been in a serious relationship since we'd ended. No matter what excuses I told the guys, she was the reason. The only reason I needed.

I loved Ella Larson, and I couldn't deny it any longer.

I held her against me, wondering if I shouldn't just tell her the truth. Otherwise, there was no way I could take her tonight in the way I wanted.

I argued with myself. Should I tell her, shouldn't I. The internal debate was driving me crazy. Would she even remember me saying anything to her? Perhaps waiting until tomorrow was better. Sober was always the better option in my book.

"Part of me wishes this was real because I know it wouldn't be a mistake," she murmured against my chest.

My eyes flew open, and panic flooded me. Did she think the ceremony was fake? I could already feel her wrath when she found out it was as real as they had come. She'd probably never speak to me again.

"You know what?"

"What?"

"I think it's time to get you into bed," I said, unwrapping her arms from around my waist and guiding her toward her room.

I'd just turned to help her down the two stairs when she wrapped her arms around my neck. "Now you are talking. Take me to bed and have your way with me," she said, reaching over and pulling at the tie my mother insisted I wore, then undoing the top two buttons on my shirt.

"Ella, what do you think you're doing?" I questioned.

She looked up at me with laughter in her eyes, which quickly turned serious when I didn't start laughing.

"Even if it is our fake wedding night, I figured you'd want..." Her voice cracked as she stopped speaking and studied me.

There it was. She really believed this had all been fake. I could only imagine what she'd do when she found out it was true.

"Lucas? Do you not want to?" she asked.

There wasn't a bone in my body that didn't want to, but before I could say anything, she tore her eyes away from mine and looked around the room. I could see the tears forming. She swallowed hard and then turned those tear-filled eyes my way.

"It's okay, I get it. It's not like I haven't been in this position before. In fact, it's been more often this position than the other." She forced a weak, embarrassed laugh.

I felt her hand slip from mine as she turned away from me and carefully climbed up the two stairs from the sunken living room to her bedroom door.

I didn't know what emotion I was feeling. What I knew was that I didn't want her to walk away from me thinking I didn't want her.

"Ella…" I called out as my voice cracked.

Only she didn't turn toward me. With her hand on the door, she stopped.

"Don't worry Lucas. I understand."

What did she understand? Before I could ask, before I could even realize what it was she thought she understood, she'd slipped in behind her bedroom door and closed it, and all I could hear were her deep sobs coming from the other side.

I LAY IN BED, staring up at the ceiling, like I'd done most of the night. The rest of it, I'd tossed and turned. I let out a sigh, then slipped from the bed, throwing on my grey sweatpants before making my way to the washroom where I splashed water on my face before heading out to make us both a coffee.

There was no doubt in my mind we needed to talk this morning. I dried my face, took a deep breath, and made my way out of my room. Her door was still closed, the lights were all off. She was probably feeling it this morning, I thought as I made my way toward the small kitchenette and flipped on the light.

I filled the coffeemaker and flipped the switch on and leaned against the counter, my mind filling once again with thoughts of us from before and now. The feeling of that first kiss, once again, then holding her in my arms the other night, then the sound of her voice as she screamed my name as she climaxed, the feeling of her nails digging into my back.

"Fuck it," I muttered and pushed myself off the counter and made my way over to her door.

Throwing the door open, the room was dark. The only light spilling in was the light from the kitchenette. Making my way over toward her bed, I sat down on the edge, gently running my hand over to where I'd expected her to be lying only to feel nothing but the bedding.

I leaned over and flipped on the light to find the bed was empty, not even slept in. I frowned and looked around for her bags, but they, too, were gone.

I frowned and got up off the bed and headed toward the bathroom, to find all her stuff gone from there too. She'd left.

I rushed out of the bedroom and to my room, grabbing my phone from my charger. There was nothing from her, or anyone for that matter. I grabbed my shirt, throwing it over my head, and took off toward the kitchen to shut off the coffeemaker.

Running toward the door, I slipped my shoes on and was about to pull the door open but stopped dead when I saw a piece of paper folded taped to the door with my name scribbled on it.

I pulled it off and opened it. As I read what she'd written, I sank to the floor. With my heart in my throat, I realized I was too late.

She was gone.

Chapter Nine

Ella - One Week Later

I SAT across from Aurora and Lorelai, sipping on my coffee while they sat there talking about some upcoming announcement at work. I was sure I'd read something in my email about earlier in the week about it but really had paid little attention.

It had probably been one of the worst weeks I'd had since I'd started working with the team. I'd called in sick for two days, and the days I was there I'd hidden in my office, refusing to see anyone. I'd monitored all my calls, weeding out any calls that came from Lucas. He'd even tried to come by and see me, but I told my assistant to tell him I was in another meeting.

"You alright, Ella?"

I looked up to see Aurora staring my way with concern.

"Yeah, just got another one of those headaches again," I lied.

I'd told them I'd been getting super odd headaches and that was why I'd been off work for two days. I wasn't sure they'd believe it, but they hadn't pushed for any more information. They'd both just wished me well.

"Maybe you should come and see one of us. Perhaps you've slept on your neck wrong," Lorelai offered.

"No, it's okay. I'm sure it will go away."

"Well, maybe just pop in and see the team doc. I mean, maybe he can give you something. You look like you are going to be sick," Aurora added.

Did I really look that bad? I was certain I'd put on enough makeup to hide the puffy eyes and dark circles.

"Anyway, Dylan and I were talking last night and he's hoping it's an announcement of some new players to replace a couple that are on the verge of leaving."

"Yeah, Knox said the same thing. He said anything would be an improvement from Johnson." Lorelai laughed.

"Hard not to be. Dylan doesn't even know how

Johnson got to where he is," Aurora agreed. "He makes me laugh."

"Sounds like something he'd say," Lorelai added.

I placed my coffee mug down and picked up my muffin, shoving almost half of it in my mouth at once. It was the first thing I'd eaten in two days; I was starving now that I was around food, and my stomach let out a grumble, thanking me for feeding it, even if it was only flour and sugar. It was then I noticed both girls looking at me.

"What?" I asked, after I'd swallowed everything in my mouth.

"You sure you're alright? You're acting as if you haven't eaten in days," Lorelai said, taking a small bite of the chocolate-covered croissant in front of her.

"Sorry, ate really early this morning," I lied.

"We asked you if you knew what the secret announcement is. I'm sure your father has mentioned something to you."

I hadn't spoken to my father since before I'd gone away with Lucas. I had no clue what the announcement was.

"Nope, not a clue. My father tells me nothing," I muttered. "And I don't really want to talk about my father."

Lorelai and Aurora looked at one another and then back to me.

"What?" I questioned, knowing they both had something on their minds.

"Ella, we are worried about you."

"Why? There is nothing wrong."

"Ella, you haven't been yourself all week, and Dylan said that you approached him about the hospital campaign to see if he would mind taking part, even though he said he was taken off the project and that your father designated Lucas as the spokesperson instead because of his knee injury."

I swallowed hard.

"Yeah, Knox mentioned something about this as well. He said that you followed him out to his car to see if he'd step back in. Does Lucas not want to take part?"

I'd panicked after I'd returned from Vegas. It had happened on Monday when I'd called in sick and then decided I'd work from home. I'd opened my email to see that the photoshoot had been rescheduled and was now set to take place at the beginning of next week instead of the weekend. Instead of emailing Lucas the details, I'd taken matters into my own hands, went against my father's instruction, and tried to get either Dylan or Knox to take part instead. They were demanding I be there for the photoshoot, and the last person I wanted to see or spend time with was Lucas.

"What's going on, Ella? We all thought Lucas was the one to get the spotlight on this? I can't imagine he'd not want to do it. After all, this sort of thing looks great for the guys," Aurora said as both girls looked at me.

I bit my bottom lip, wondering just how much I should divulge.

"We both know he can be difficult with these things," Lorelai said.

"Maybe we can help," Aurora said. "We can always talk to the boys and have them talk to him."

"It's not that. He's more than happy to do it," I muttered, my finger tracing the rim of my mug.

"We don't understand. Why are you asking the others to do it if he isn't refusing?"

I sighed and then looked at the girls with defeat. "Look, I've not mentioned this to many people. Actually, I haven't mentioned this to anyone at work, but Lucas and I…"

"Oh my god, are you guys dating?" Aurora questioned, almost ready to jump out of her seat with excitement.

"Oh gosh, how did I not see this?" Lorelai exclaimed.

"No…" I almost screamed, putting an end to that before it could even start.

"Then what is it?" Lorelai questioned.

I let out a sigh. "We dated years ago. It's just an uncomfortable situation."

"What? How did we not know this?" Aurora questioned.

"Because I said nothing."

"Well, I knew there had to be something between the pair of you," Lorelai added. "Especially after the night in the locker room."

"You did?" I questioned.

"Yeah, we figured you were secretly dating, especially when Knox and Dylan saw the two of you at the airport together last Friday," Lorelai said.

I frowned. "What do you mean?"

"Well, when we didn't go out last weekend and we mentioned you weren't feeling well, that was when Dylan said he saw the pair of you at the airport," Aurora said, sipping her coffee.

"Yeah, we figured you didn't want us to know, so we didn't press the issue. Thought we'd back off and you could tell us when you were ready," Lorelai added.

I was about to deny it when my phone vibrated against the table, and I looked down to see Lucas's name on the screen. He hadn't given up; he was still trying to get a hold of me. When I looked up, I knew both of them had seen it as well.

"It's not what you think," I said, sending his call to voicemail.

"Uh-huh, sneaking away to be together. We know exactly how it is." Lorelai giggled.

"No, honestly, it wasn't like that. I did him a favor, helped him with a family problem," I answered.

"Let me guess, the girlfriend issue?" Aurora asked.

I looked over at her in shock. "How did you know that?"

"He'd been complaining to the boys about it one night when I was working on his knee. From what he was saying, his mother can be quite persistent, and while he'd been able to avoid going to see his mother since she moved to Vegas, once he got injured, he couldn't avoid it any longer. He even begged both Dylan and Knox to borrow one of us just to shut her up."

"Yeah, Knox loved that." Lorelai giggled. "He basically told Lucas if he ever asked him that question again, he'd take him out on the ice during a game."

"Funny, Dylan said the same thing." Aurora laughed. "It was nice of you to help him out. Did it go okay?"

I smiled for the first time in a week, thinking about how the weekend had started, but that quickly faded when I remembered how it had ended.

"Yeah, I mean, I think we made his mother happy. She invited me for Christmas."

"So now what happens?

"What do you mean?"

"Well, obviously, his mother thinks the two of you are together. What's going to happen now? Is Lucas just going to tell her you guys split?"

I shrugged. "I'm guessing at some point he is going to tell her we got divorced before the holidays."

"Divorced?" Lorelai questioned. "Why would he tell her that?"

"Well, his sisters and mother wouldn't let up on either of us, so somehow we ended up taking part in a fake ceremony at one of those wedding chapels on the strip."

Aurora and Lorelai looked at one another then back over at me with wide eyes.

"Why are you two looking at me like that?" I questioned, shoving the rest of my muffin into my mouth.

"Uh, Ella, you know those places aren't fake, right?" Lorelai questioned.

"Yes, they are."

They both glanced at one another, a worried look on their face and then turned back to me.

"What do you mean?" I said, panic filling me.

"They are real."

"No, they aren't," I said, swallowing hard. "Please stop trying to make me panic." I laughed nervously.

"Sorry to break it to you but they are…thousands

of people run off to Vegas every year to get married. How do you not know this?"

"Yeah, I know that, but not at the one we went to. I mean, there were so many pictures of celebrity weddings that I recognized from movies. Plus, it was so commercialized there was no way it could have been real."

"What was the name of the place?" Aurora asked.

"Um, gosh, Moments at Midnight, or something like that," I said, playing with the muffin wrapper.

"Midnight Moments?" Aurora corrected. "Is that the one?"

"Yeah, that is it!"

"It's real. Dylan and I looked at sneaking off to Vegas one night just to take all the pressure off. With him trying to repair his relationship with his father and, well, the relationship between my mother and Dylan's dad, things haven't been easy."

"We wouldn't blame you, you know. Not with lil baby dominator on the way," Lorelai said, reaching over and rubbing Aurora's belly.

"No, there is no way. It's not real," I said, panic filling me.

It was then I felt a hand on my shoulder and heard his voice. "It's real, Ella."

I whipped around as both the girls looked up and saw Lucas standing behind me.

"Hey, Lucas," Aurora and Lorelai said in unison.

"Hey, ladies, do you mind if I have a chat with Ella?"

"No, not at all. We were just leaving," they both said, scooting out of the bench seat on the other side of the booth.

I looked over at both of them, practically begging them with my eyes not to leave, but it did little good. They already had their purses flung over their shoulders and were almost at the door.

"We'll call you later," they called, looking over their shoulder at us.

Lucas waited until they'd left the Sip and Stir and then slipped into the bench seat across from me.

"It was real?" I said, swallowing hard.

Lucas nodded. "It was."

"You mean we are really married?" I said, swallowing hard.

"Yes, but that isn't why I'm here."

"It's not?"

Lucas shook his head and pulled his phone from his pocket, placing it down on the table to where I saw a message from both Knox and Dylan.

"I'm here because I want to know why you are trying to replace me for the charity thing."

I sat there, looking at him. "I don't think my trying to replace you is the most important thing here."

"I do," he said, meeting my eyes.

We stared at one another for a moment, then I shrugged. "I guess I didn't think you'd be interested in doing the event after the weekend." I mumbled.

"I promised you, didn't I?"

I nodded my head. "You did."

"Then?"

"Then what?"

"Then why are you going behind my back trying to replace me."

"Like I said, I didn't think you'd follow through. I haven't even heard from you since we came back."

"Whoa, hold on a minute. I've tried to get a hold of you, and don't you dare say I haven't. I have every single record of every phone call I've made to you in the past week."

I tore my eyes away from him. I didn't want to deal with any of this right now.

"So, tell me, why are you trying to replace me?"

"Like I said, I assumed you'd just leave me high and dry."

Lucas looked at me and shook his head. "You really need to stop assuming things."

"I don't assume things."

"You do, you just said you did."

"Lucas, I'm not—"

"What did you assume the last night in Vegas? Why did you leave?"

I balled up the wrapper from my muffin and shoved it into my coffee mug, throwing my purse strap over my head.

"I assumed nothing. I made an ass of myself, and I realized it after I went into my room. I knew there was no way I'd be able to face you in the morning, after realizing the things I said to you and that you didn't want things to move forward."

"Ella, you didn't make an ass of yourself. I should have said something to you that night, but when I looked at the situation at hand, you'd had a lot to drink, and now that I know for a fact that you thought the wedding thing was fake, I'm glad I listened to my myself and pursued nothing that night."

I didn't want to talk about that night or any night that happened during that weekend. What I really wanted was to turn back time. That way I'd not have to face Lucas, or the memory of the entire situation.

"Lucas, I'm glad you listened to yourself, and you can say whatever you want about me and that night, but I know the truth. If you are fine doing the promotion, then great. I will make sure I send you the address you'll need to be at on Monday morning."

"Okay. Will I see you there?"

I shook my head. "No."

"Why not?" he questioned, staring at me. "I believe you are supposed to be there. After all, you are representing me. If there is a problem, I can't say anything."

"It will be fine. They will have my number. Should a problem arise, they can call me, or you can."

"Ella, I'm pretty sure you are supposed to be accessible at all these types of events."

"Pamela approved it. You don't need to worry," I said, meeting his eyes.

Lucas gave me a questioning look. I knew full well I was supposed to be present at these types of things. I'd not mentioned a word to Pamela about any such thing.

"What are you going to do if you aren't there?" he asked.

"Well, this weekend I am going to take the time to find someone who will annul this marriage, and then I'm going to make sure that I message your mother and your sisters, explain the whole situation to them, and apologize to them for playing along with this crazy thing. Don't you worry, I'll take the heat on it. Then, I am going to sit down and write my resignation letter and take it to my father on Monday afternoon."

"WHAT?" Lucas exclaimed. "Are you out of your mind?"

"No, I've just given things lots of thought over the last week. As much as I love what I do, I don't think this is the place to do it in. So, with that said, I've decided that it's time for me to move on to something else."

"Ella. Do nothing rash. Think it through."

"I have, Lucas. I've given it a tremendous amount of thought."

I gathered my things, throwing my purse over my neck and adjusting it before grabbing my garbage.

"Ella."

I stopped and looked at Lucas. If I had to look at those eyes one more time I would buckle, I knew it. They were my weakness; he was my weakness.

"What?"

"Before you do anything, you need to know—"

"It's okay, Lucas. I don't need to know anything," I said, placing my hand on his. "I want you to know that I thank you for this, actually. You've given me the gift I think I've been searching for."

"What gift is that?" he questioned.

I thought for a minute, on how to explain this to him, then looked over at him. I didn't want this to come across wrong, especially knowing how he felt about me. It wasn't his fault he didn't have feelings for me. Yet I still wanted to make sure he knew he'd given me something great.

"Lucas, because of this crazy weekend, you gave me the courage to look inside my life and see what has and hasn't been working for me. You know, I always thought I didn't want to get married, to have kids, all because of what my friends have gone through and are going through, but you changed that. The idea, when presented, about getting married, actually sounded fun, and until finding out only a few minutes ago that we actually tied the knot, I'd had a blast with it. Maybe it was because I thought it was fake, I don't know but it made me realize I'd only been feeling that way about marriage because I haven't met the one yet, and I was jealous of my friends. Now, at least I know that when I meet the one, the idea of being tied to him forever won't freak me out.

"It also gave me a chance to look at my job. I'm not happy here. While I know Dad was trying to help, it was never my choice to work for my father. I want to pave my way, and I have you to thank for that, too. If it hadn't of been for you always making fun of me, well, I guess I'd have just settled and stayed on board."

"But, Ella, you can't just leave."

"Why not? This fundraiser was the only job that was assigned to me so far this year."

"Yes, because it's an important one, and it required all of your focus to make sure it went well."

"Yes, and Dad probably only handed it to me to see if I'd crack under the pressure before he gave me anything else to do. So, before he gives me anything else, it's the perfect time to announce my departure.

We will get this silly marriage annulled, and once that's done, I'll be free, and there will be nothing keeping me here."

Lucas sat there watching me, a look of disappointment on his face. He said nothing, just sat there, and after a few moments, he stood up.

"I'll look into the annulment. No need for you to worry about it. I'll take care of everything, including my mother. This isn't on you, never was, and I won't let it be now. I am sorry I put you in this position. You focus on your letter of resignation and, if you could, please text me the address of where I need to be on Monday."

He looked down at me, placed his hand on top of mine, and gave me a smile that didn't reach his eyes. "Good luck on whatever path you decide."

I studied his eyes, he was crushed, and it pulled at my heart like nothing ever had before. I was about to say something, but he'd already taken his hand from mine, turned away, and was heading out the doors of the Sip and Stir.

It seriously felt as if we'd broken up all over again.

I picked up my cup and threw it in the trash, then made my way out of the little shop and started walking toward my apartment. I thought after sharing my plans with Lucas I'd feel lighter than ever, but instead, my chest hurt, and my body felt heavy. I couldn't go through this again. I needed to focus and get my life in order. After all, this was what I wanted, wasn't it?

Once I got home, I sat down and began writing my resignation while thinking about things. I soon realized that maybe, just maybe, this wasn't what I wanted, and I'd rushed into this decision too.

Chapter Ten

Lucas - One Week Later

I'D COMPLETED the photoshoot without issue, as promised, but still hadn't seen or spoken to Ella since the Sip and Stir. I glanced down at my watch, threw my sweatshirt over my head, and took off toward the boardroom.

Dylan, Knox, and Clay sat with the rest of the team as I walked in and took my seat. Coach Thompkins called this meeting late last night. We'd all got an email from Pamela, the head of PR, telling us to attend. It was mentioned that Guy Larson would attend as well. It was rare that Larson came to any player meeting, and with that information we knew there was an important announcement coming.

"Where the hell have you been?" I asked Clay, as I pulled my chair over closer to the guys.

Clay had been scarce the last few weeks and had been oddly quiet when we'd contacted him. I was worried about him, and so were the other guys, but we didn't like to push. He was a private guy, and we all knew he'd come around when he was ready.

"None of your concern," he muttered, flipping through his phone as Dylan and Knox glanced over at him and frowned.

"Okay then. Do you guys know why we've been brought in here? I have things I need to do today."

"Don't we all," Knox said, sending off a text message to I assumed was Lorelai.

"Word has it we are getting some new players," Dylan said, looking up just as Coach Thompkins and Guy Larson entered the room, followed by Pamela.

Everyone stilled as they made their way to the front of the table, placing some papers down in front of them before talking amongst themselves. I couldn't read the expressions on anyone's face to know whether it was good news or bad. There were more words exchanged, and then they turned their attention to all of us.

"Good morning, gentlemen," Thompkins said,

filling the glass in front of him with water. "Good practice this morning."

The entire team sat there, quietly, waiting to find out exactly what was going on.

"We won't keep you in suspense any longer. As you know, we've been short of a couple of players. Stanton and Whittaker are both out as of last month, which means we've been looking for new players. After some crazy negotiations, we want to announce to you the players that will join the Dominators."

I looked at my teammates as we sat there waiting for the names of the players.

"The players are Colton Fox and Levi Anderson."

My head jerked up after the announcement of our new team mates. While Levi Anderson was a solid player coming from the New York Predators and would be an amazing addition to the Dominators, Colton Fox was another story. He was hell on skates, a skilled player but a bad boy, both on and off the ice, with an extensive track record to prove it. No doubt the Boston Enforcers saw an opportunity to rid themselves of a player with a troublemaker attitude.

I glanced over at Dylan, Knox, and Clay, each of us saying with our eyes what someone should have said to Larson with this decision. It was then Pamela leaned over and whispered something to Larson. I watched as he nodded, then looked at each of us.

"I know you are probably worried about Colton Fox bringing a bad rap to the team, but rest assured, he's cleaned up his act."

I glanced at the boys, who just shook their heads. Colton Fox had done nothing of the sort. The last game he played should have proved that, but apparently Larson was blind.

"Thompkins, if you have anything else to add, I'd take this opportunity now, otherwise let them head home and get ready to leave tonight. I have to go meet with my daughter."

At the mention of Ella, I sat up a little. I wondered if she'd told her father she was leaving the team already, or if she was about to do it now. Either way, knowing she was in the building at this moment sent a wave of excitement through me. All that ran through my mind were the things I needed to talk to her about.

I watched as Larson left the room and Thompkins stepped into his place. He stood in front of us, looking at each one of us. Of all days, today was the only day I didn't want to stay in some blasted meeting.

"Alright, guys, I will not keep you. Why don't you all head home? Be back here for three, ready to head off for our games in Florida. Oh, and Clark, you're coming with the team tonight. Got word you've been cleared to start playing again. We already have plans in place for this game, so we will keep you as backup."

I nodded as I glanced at my watch. It was already eleven. If I was going to talk to Ella, make it home to pack and get back to the arena, I'd have to move fast.

"Anybody wanna go get lunch?" Dylan questioned as we all stood up. "I have a craving for The Sushi Garden," he said, patting his stomach.

"You've always got a craving for that," Clay muttered, "but I'm down. Knox? Lucas?"

"Yep, count me in," Knox answered.

"I have a meeting I have to attend first with the therapist," I lied.

"Uh-huh," Knox and Dylan said in unison, causing Clay to look at them in question.

"He's working his magic with some chick, which he still hasn't filled us in about, but we'll fill you in with the information we have. Perhaps we'll make some shit up as well. Let's go."

I took off down the hall toward the main offices in search of Ella while the guys went for lunch, where there was no doubt in my mind, I'd be the major topic of conversation.

I ROUNDED the corner in time to see Ella disappear into her father's office. I'd have figured I'd be able to beat her to the office and stop her from making a huge mistake.

I continued down the hall and stopped just outside of Larson's door. The door was open a crack, and I could hear him talking—well, yelling, like he always did.

"Daddy, I didn't come here to talk about my next assignment. I came here to tell you I am resigning from my current position," I heard Ella say.

I stood there, waiting to hear what Larson was going to say. The office was quiet; I imagined them standing there, staring at one another in some sort of father-daughter showdown.

"Ella, what are you talking about?" he questioned in that stern voice I hated.

"This isn't the job for me, Daddy."

"Ella, what exactly is for you? You never follow through with anything. You begged me for this position, and I gave you exactly what you wanted. I should have known better because you never stick with anything."

"I gave it a chance. I can't help it if it's not for me."

"Ella, you should know that if you walk away from this, there is no more coming back to me."

"I know, and I don't plan to come back to you."

"Until the next plan doesn't work out so well. It's a pattern with you. You don't think I already know that you'll be back here, begging me for another chance."

Ella really did not know what it was she was giving up. A solid job with a solid team. She couldn't be that irresponsible.

"It's because of Clark, isn't it?" I heard Larson question. "You're leaving because of him. When are you going to get that through your head, Ella?"

"This has nothing to do with Lucas, Daddy."

"I'll be the decider of that."

I stood there for a moment and was about to knock on the door to stop this craziness when the door was abruptly pulled open, and I stood face-to-face with Guy Larson.

"Well, well, look who it is…Clark, get your ass in here."

"Sir?" I muttered.

"Don't sir me. Get in here," he said, stepping to the side.

The moment he stepped to the side, my eyes met Ella's. She stood there with her mouth agape.

"Don't drag Lucas into this, Daddy. This is my decision," Ella said.

Only Larson didn't stop. Instead, he shut the door and then moved to his chair behind his desk.

"Until Lucas got injured, everything was fine.

You'd been working side by side with both Dylan and Knox on the hospital fundraiser. Things were good, you were succeeding in your position. Then your entire demeanor changed when I pulled them off the promotion and put Lucas in their place. Within a day, your work slipped, your attitude toward everything went downhill to the point you requested a weekend off because you could no longer handle the stress of the workload. I won't say I didn't worry about the fact that your ex-boyfriend was a player on the team, especially after the time it took you to get over him, and now you want to quit. You can't tell me it isn't because of him," Larson said, glancing in my direction.

"Daddy, really, just stop. I didn't have any issues getting over him."

"Ella, honestly. You can't even be honest with yourself. You think I don't hear you talking with your friends? You don't think I see the sideways glances you give him, or the longing look in your eyes each time he's mentioned. There is nothing to be ashamed of Ella, you love the man."

"Seriously, Daddy, stop."

"Truth hurts, doesn't it?"

I glanced over at Ella. I could tell she was on the verge of tears.

"Can I speak with you outside for a moment?" I said, leaning toward her.

She didn't tear her eyes from her father; she just stood there staring back at him. I had to do something before she fucked up her entire life by telling him off and quitting her job.

"Ella?" I whispered, reaching out and placing my hand on her arm, trying to get her to look at me.

"No," she said, her eyes still trained on her father.

"Ella, for once, be wise. Go talk with him," Larson said, pulling his chair out and sitting down, placing his attention on his computer screen.

Ella stomped her foot, let out a huff, and then marched out of his office. I took off after her without another word, pulling her father's door closed behind me.

"What do you want, Lucas?" she asked, her back to me, her arms crossed in front of her as she stared out the fourth-floor window. "I am trying to resign."

"Don't be stupid, Ella. Don't throw away an amazing career. You are great at what you do."

"That might be, but I am just here because my father got me the job, remember? At least that is what you've always said, and it appears you are right."

"I never meant it. I only said that to get under your skin."

"Well, mission accomplished." She sniffled.

"Look, I'm sorry. I never thought you'd take those

words to heart. I used to bust your ass all the time when we dated."

"Well, I was a different person then."

"What changed?" I asked.

"What didn't?" she said, rubbing her upper arms as if she were cold. "Anyway, what was it you wanted to talk to me about that couldn't wait?" she asked, finally turning to me.

I'd said that just to pull her out of the situation. What I needed and wanted to say really should be said when we were out of earshot of her father.

"It can wait," I said, crossing my arms in front of my chest.

She gave me an irritated look and made her way over to me. I moved in front of the door to her father's office, blocking her. She stopped and, with her jaw clenched, she met my eyes.

"Lucas, get out of my way."

"Ella, I will not stand here and allow you to make the biggest mistake of your life. This job is you. We need you here."

"Lucas, please, the Dominators will be fine without me. Now please…" she said, pushing past me.

She was just about to push open her father's door when panic flooded me.

"Dominators may be fine without you, but I won't be," I said.

"Lucas, now isn't the time for this."

"I'm serious, Ella."

"Lucas, please, next thing you're going to tell me is that you didn't get someone to annul this stupid marriage," she said loud enough I was certain her father would hear.

Had I found someone? I had, I'd kept my word. Had I booked an appointment for us? I'd done that too.

"When?" she asked, turning toward me, her back to her father's office door.

"When what?" I questioned, just as her father's office door opened and he stood there staring at me.

Instead of making eye contact with him, I continued to stare at Ella.

"Lucas, when is the annulment?" she demanded.

It was wrong of me not to stop her, but she needed to know I was serious about my feelings, and if this was the only way I was going to prove to her I was serious, fuck it. I'd take my life in my hands.

I didn't need to look away from her; I knew her father was staring at me. I also knew he was going to kill me.

"Annulment? What annulment?" Larson questioned.

Ella spun around and looked at her father, and

then back at me, her eyes horrified and then filling with tears.

"Why would you have just stood there and not told me he was there?" she said through clenched teeth.

"Ella, I demand answers," Larson said, looking between the two of us.

Larson's eyes drilled right into me as he stood there waiting for a response from one of us.

Ella was like a deer in headlights. She looked first at her dad, then at me, then back to him, not saying a word.

"So, just as I figured. He had something to do with it. You're not resigning, and I want an explanation right this minute. What the fuck is going on here?"

I looked over at Ella. She looked like she was on the verge of a panic attack; she was pale, and her chest was rising and falling in rapid succession.

"I...I can't do this..." she muttered and took off down the hall, not looking back at either of us. Instead of following her, I turned back to her father, met his eyes, and stepped forward.

"What do you have to say for yourself this time, Clark?" he questioned.

"I have nothing to say, but I think we should talk."

I pushed past him and entered his office, pacing back and forth while I waited for him to close his office door.

Chapter Eleven

Ella - Sunday Night

I STARED AT MY PHONE, the email from my father causing my stomach to roll. He'd put it in writing and had sent a copy to Human Resources, notifying them he refused to accept my resignation. Anger flooded me as I stared at my screen.

"Can I help you?" I heard and looked up to see the girl behind the counter at Sip and Stir staring back at me.

"Coffee, black please," I demanded.

"Size?"

Ignoring her, I hit reply to the email.

"Miss, what size would you like?"

"Large," I said, letting out a huff.

I'd been in a mood the entire weekend, ever since running out of the arena on Friday. I'd left my father and Lucas standing there in the hallway staring at one another and had locked myself in my apartment, ignoring all calls and messages the entire weekend.

I tapped my card and then moved down the counter and grabbed my coffee from another girl, making my way out of the shop and heading back home. I stopped at the corner, glancing at the text messages that had come in over the weekend.

Aurora, Lorelai, and Layla had all messaged a couple of times, but Lucas had blown up my messages ever since Friday night. It had been so bad I'd had to shut my volume off.

I shook my head as I stared at his name. Seventeen messages over the course of the weekend. You'd have thought that when a few of them hadn't been read he'd stop sending them. The man was persistent if not anything else.

The moment the light changed, I shoved my phone in my pocket and made my way across the street, stopping in at the small grocery store for some things. I'd lived on cold pizza for the past two days and needed something a little healthier for dinner tonight, and something for lunches for the week because, apparently, I had to go to work.

I gathered a few things, paid for them, and then left, making my way around the corner to the condo. Out of the corner of my eye, I saw someone standing at the front door of the building, but since I didn't want to be bothered, I didn't make eye contact. Instead, I dug my hand into my pocket and pulled out my keys, opening the front door.

"Ella…" I heard a familiar voice say from behind me.

I stopped, closed my eyes, took a deep breath, and then glanced over my shoulder. Lucas stood there, dressed in his grey sweatpants and his Dominators sweatshirt he always wore when returning from an away game. He looked tired, even stressed.

"What do you want?" I asked.

I was angry he'd not come to me after I'd left. It just went to prove exactly what I thought. I'd peeked at the messages he'd left, not one of them telling me what date he'd set for our annulment, which had led me to believe he'd not really booked one.

"Can we go inside?" he asked, grabbing the door and opening it for me.

With my hands full, struggling to hold onto the two full bags of groceries I'd picked up, I couldn't argue.

"Fine," I said, moving through the door and quickly pressing the elevator button.

Neither one of us said anything until we were both inside the condo. He'd held that door open for me too, letting me inside first, and I'd immediately gone to the kitchen and shoved things into the fridge, then turned to find him standing in the doorway watching me.

"I tried messaging you over the weekend," he said, his eyes meeting mine.

I let out a sigh. "I know, I saw."

"Did you read them?" he questioned, leaning up against the doorframe.

I shook my head. Hell, why did he have to always look so good when he came back from a game? Those sexy ass messy curls, t-shirt stretched in all the right places, and those grey sweatpants that hung off his hips, had always made my mouth water.

"Why not?"

I got up from the table. There was no way I could sit here staring at him any longer. I began pulling out bowls and measuring cups, then started pulling out ingredients to make some muffins.

"I wanted to be alone for the weekend," I muttered, concentrating on what I was doing as I added two cups of flour to the bowl.

"What does reading my messages have to do with

that? You could have read them; I wasn't asking for a response."

"Why? So, I could hear all about you and my father having it out, then about you losing your position and knowing that it was my fault. My father already thinks he knows that my wanting to quit has to do with you, which he is wrong about that. The last thing I need to hear is that all your hard work has been thrown down the drain because of me. My father can be the biggest asshole when he wants to teach me a lesson."

"Do you honestly think your father could get rid of me that easy?"

"I do, he's the boss."

"I see. Well, I have lawyers, you know. They seem to have more of a final say than your father. He may not want me on the team, but I can assure you he's the one who would have to suck it up."

"Trust me when I say he'd get the final word. He always does," I muttered, still irritated from the email he'd sent earlier.

Lucas was quiet, almost like he wasn't even here. I added some sugar to the bowl and went to grab the milk when I felt his hands on my arms. I stopped, afraid to move, knowing if I backed up an inch I'd feel his body behind mine. I could already feel the heat from his body as I stood there.

"Why didn't you read my messages?" he whispered.

I closed my eyes. He already knew how I felt. It was almost as if he wanted to torture me, by making me answer this question.

"Lucas, I…"

My eyes were burning as I stopped speaking and swallowed hard. I felt like I could cry and be sick all at the same time.

"Open my messages," he said, quietly, nothing more than a whisper as he picked up my phone and placed it in front of me. "Just read what I had to say to you."

He didn't step back to give me space, the heat from his body was enveloping me now, making me warmer than what I already was as anxiousness filled me. I took a deep breath and, with a shaking hand, picked up my phone, opening the messages from Lucas. It took me a minute to find the first one he'd sent.

I read through the first sixteen, they'd all been the same, asking me to message, or call when I got the message. It was the seventeenth that caught my attention just as I was going to stop reading them.

Lucas: Ella, I'm sorry about everything. Everything has blown way out of control. First, I really did think you knew that all weddings that take place in Vegas were real. I did abide by your wishes and line up someone to annul our marriage, so there is no need to worry. Before that, though, there are things I want to say. I stood there Friday, outside your father's office, wishing I could just tell you how I felt. Just like I wanted to the night after the ceremony, but you were drunk, and you were too inside your own head to listen. I know that because I see you. The real you, the one you hide from everyone. It was the same on Friday. I knew if I started to tell you how I felt, you'd shut me out, so instead I took matters into my own hands. That was why I said nothing while your father stood behind you and I allowed you to question me. I figured it was the only way you'd know I was serious, by taking my life into my own hands, otherwise you'd never believe me. Your father can be one scary guy, and this is coming from a six-foot, 208 lbs. guy. I told your father everything, and you need to know that I'm in love with you and have been for as long as I can remember. It just took reconnecting to make me realize it, and while I know you want to annul this marriage, I beg of you to take a minute, stop, step outside of your own head and remember what we had. Msg me when you get this, please, don't make me wait.

. . .

I STOOD THERE, staring at the message on my phone. I could still feel the warmth of his body behind mine, which let me know he hadn't moved away from me. I swallowed hard as the message blurred, tears filling my eyes. I had to remind myself to breathe and placed my phone on the counter. Everything I'd thought was wrong.

"Say something," he whispered. "Don't make me wait any longer."

I inhaled deeply, trying to do as he asked, which was get out of my own head, even for a moment. That had always been something I'd struggled with. I'd always come to my own conclusions, no matter what others said, and I always jumped into everything without thinking of the consequences. Perhaps this time, I should take his advice and shut off that inner voice for a moment.

"I'm still in love with you. Did you read that?" he whispered.

I leaned back against him, allowing the heat from him to envelop me, thinking back to the first night in Vegas, remembering everything. I'd not seen it, even though the morning after we'd been together, he'd clearly been trying to tell me how he felt. He just didn't know how to get the words out, but he'd still tried. I just figured he was saying the words I wanted to hear, so I didn't start regretting what had happened that night.

I closed my eyes and turned to face him, and slowly looked up at him, almost immediately crashing into him.

"I'm so sorry," I cried. "I couldn't see it."

"It's okay," he said, his voice low as he wrapped his arms around me.

"No, it's not. I pushed you away because I thought I knew it all."

"You have to shove harder than that to push me away, Ella."

I snuggled against his chest, my heart finally feeling at peace for the first time in a long time.

"How did my father take it?" I questioned, looking up at Lucas.

The sexy, shit-eating grin Lucas always wore whenever I'd mention my father appeared on his lips.

"Let's just say he gave us his blessing."

He lowered his head, bringing his lips to mine, wrapping his arms around me tighter as he deepened the kiss.

My fingers ran through his hair as his tongue washed through my mouth. My body heated as his hands ran over my body, his hands gripping my ass and pulling me closer to him.

"I want you…I want all of you." I moaned between kisses. In one swift motion, he placed his hands under my legs, picked me up, and carried me down to my bedroom.

Kissing me, he gently lowered me to the floor, gripped the hem of my shirt, and lifted it over my head, dropping it to the floor. Pulling at the button on my jeans, he pushed those to my feet and knelt down in front of me, my fingers running through his hair as he placed a kiss on my lower abdomen and looked up at me.

"I can't wait to take you and make you mine," he whispered as he looked up at me.

I stared into his eyes, heat coursing through my body as his fingers danced gently up the back of my legs.

"Make me yours," I moaned as I closed my eyes and dropped my head back at the feeling of his fingers as they slid between my legs, sliding through my center.

"Turn around, bend over, support yourself with your arms."

A wave of excitement ran through me as I did as he asked. I felt him tap my inner leg, and I parted my legs, feeling him run his tongue through my slit as he grabbed my ass.

"This pussy…all of it…is mine," he growled, lightly tapping my right cheek.

Excitement filled me, making it hard for me to breathe as I felt him line himself up at my entrance and bury himself inside of me. I closed my eyes, a loud moan escaping my lips as he began thrusting as he held onto my hips, pushing me over the edge.

Chapter Twelve

Lucas - Two Weeks Later

"LAST BAG UNPACKED," Ella said, coming out of the bedroom and sitting down on the stool at the breakfast bar.

She reached over and grabbed a cracker off the charcuterie board I'd just placed out and smiled at me.

"Sure you're ready?" I asked, passing her a bottle of water.

"I think so," she said, looking down at the diamond ring that now sat on her finger.

It had been the first thing I'd done the morning after I took my wife for the first time.

"Do you think they will be ready?" she asked, looking at me and then back down to the ring.

Tonight, I'd invited the guys over for a little team party after we won our last home game. We had a few days off, and I figured it would be a good time to let them know about Ella and me. We'd both promised one another that we wouldn't say anything to anyone until tonight, after Ella had moved in.

"I think so," she said, looking up at me, worry in her eyes.

"What's that look for?" I questioned.

"There's no look." She smiled, looking back at the ring on her finger.

"Do you not like it?" I questioned, turning to the fridge to pull out the appetizers Ella had made a few hours ago.

"Do I not like what?" she questioned, reaching over and grabbing another cracker.

"The ring, you keep looking at it. If you don't like it, we can always return it and you can choose something else," I said, unwrapping the board.

"Are you kidding me? I love it. Guess I'm just getting used to it, and I'll be happy that starting tomorrow I can wear it all the time." She giggled, getting up off the stool, coming around the counter and wrapping her arms around me, playing with the curls at the back of my head.

I stared into her eyes. I could see nothing but playfulness in them as she stared up at me. I lowered my mouth to hers, teasing her and kissing her lightly.

"Don't start," I murmured, closing my eyes as I felt her hand run over my semi-hard cock.

"Why not? Why not take me right here, on the counter?" she whispered.

When I looked at her eyes, I saw nothing but want in them.

"You want me to take you on the counter? Right here? Make you my own personal appetizer?" I whispered, grazing her lips with mine.

Her chest rose and fell in quick succession, and she swallowed hard as I ran my fingers over her bottom lip. God, I wanted to take her right here right now, but I knew it would only be a minute or two before the boys were here.

I felt her hands on my stomach, running up under my shirt and back down over my abs, stopping at the button on my jeans. I closed my eyes and leaned back against the counter, when a pounding knock brought me out of the moment.

Ella looked up at me, disappointment lining her face as she glanced over at the door. "Guess they are here."

"Yep," I said, removing her hands from the button on my jeans and adjusting myself. "Be prepared for later, you little tease," I said as I nipped her mouth with mine.

I made my way over and opened the door, welcoming Dylan and Aurora, Knox and Lorelai, and Clay.

"You all know Ella," I said, as they all came in and removed their shoes.

Aurora and Lorelai both smiled in her direction and immediately went over to her talking about last night's win.

"So, what's this news you got for us?" Dylan asked, placing a case of beer on the counter.

"Yeah, come on, we want to know. You've kept us in suspense long enough," Knox added.

"I haven't." I chuckled.

"Bullshit. Care to talk about the text messages from a few weeks ago?"

I walked over to Ella and wrapped my arm around her as all of them looked on.

"What?" Aurora and Lorelai both said at the same time. "No way!"

Ella looked at them and smiled while nodding her head.

"What?" Knox asked at the same time Clay did.

It was then I took hold of Ella's hand in mine, raising it up to show them the ring.

"Jesus…" Knox groaned. "This is the girl…and your married?"

Lorelai let out a little giggle as Knox ran his hands over his face in shock.

"It's not good, Lorelai, it's the boss's daughter… Jesus. We can't afford to lose Lucas," Knox grunted.

I glanced down at Ella and winked while Knox started pacing the kitchen floor.

"What's the problem?" Dylan questioned, leaning up against the counter, pulling Aurora in front of him as he rested his hands on her small baby bump.

"Larson is going to go postal when he finds out. Remember what happened over the locker room incident? We almost lost him then. What do you think he's going to do when he finds this out? We need a plan, and we need a plan now!"

It was then I laughed. I'd never seen Knox this panicked before. Normally, he was a go-with-the-flow kind of guy. Clay stood there, his arms crossed across his chest, not saying a word.

"Larson won't say anything. He already knows," I said as Knox spun around and looked me directly in the eyes. "Ella and I used to date, years ago."

"Why didn't you tell us?"

"Better to watch your ass panic." I chuckled.

"Oh fuck off," Knox gritted.

I frowned. "What the hell is the matter with you?" I questioned, as Dylan and Clay looked over at Knox in shock.

We all waited as Knox glanced at all of us. "It's Peyton, my mom emailed me."

"Why didn't you tell me?" Lorelai questioned, looking concerned.

"Didn't want to talk about it." He shrugged.

It was then Clay cleared his throat and mentioned that he forgot something in the car, and before we could say anything, he'd bolted from the condo.

"I need to go out there on our next days off." Knox added, "I just don't have the bandwidth to deal with it right now, and then this news just catapulted me I guess."

"Oh, honey," Lorelai said, moving over to where he stood. "Whatever it is, I'll help you deal with it," she assured him, placing a kiss on his lips.

"Sorry, dude, didn't mean to rain on your parade," Knox said, fist bumping me.

"No worries. It would be impossible for anything to piss me off."

"Are you happy?" Aurora asked, looking over at Ella.

She rested her head on my chest and smiled. "Very."

"Well, you look better, and you've returned to your normal self. Lorelai and I were just saying that to one another yesterday at work." She smiled. "We figured things got sorted."

"So, when did this happen?" Dylan questioned.

"It was Vegas, wasn't it?" Knox asked.

I nodded. "It was. The best fucking trip to Vegas I've ever had."

It was then the door opened, and Clay came in. I noticed he had nothing with him and said nothing. Something was going on with him. I just hadn't had the time to figure out what it was.

Aurora and Lorelai came over and hugged Ella, followed by Clay, Dylan, and then finally Knox.

"Welcome to the family, darlin'," Clay said.

"Yeah, if this ass doesn't treat you right, just come to me," Dylan said, hugging her next, then smacking me across the abs.

"Yeah, we'll keep him straight," Knox added.

I walked over and cracked open the case of beer, handing out beers to the guys and then to Lorelai and Ella, then I reached into the fridge and pulled out a Gatorade for Aurora, passing it to her after I opened it.

"Let's allow the boys to chat," Aurora said, leading Ella out of the kitchen.

She turned and waved to me as the girls went into

the living room and sat on the couch. While the guys congratulated me, and we moved onto talks about upcoming games, I couldn't help but watch as the girls and Ella started talking and laughing. They'd welcome her with open arms, as would my team members. I knew that completely.

I SHUT the light off in the kitchen and made my way down to the bedroom. The soft glow from the light on my side of the bed cast enough of a glow for me to see Ella's face as she slept. I took a moment to watch her. She was so fucking beautiful, always had been to me, and now I got to call her mine.

It had taken us a few years to get this right between us, but it looked like we finally had. I was forever grateful to have her in my arms again and knew I'd never let her go. It had been a crazy few weeks, and I couldn't wait to see how crazy things were going to get in the coming years.

"You coming to bed?" I heard her murmur as she tapped the empty spot beside her.

"I'm coming, baby," I said, hitting the switch and crawling into bed beside her, pulling her against me.

"So warm," she whispered, interlocking her hand with mine.

"I love you," I said, placing a kiss on the side of her neck. "Now, where were we before we were interrupted?"

Ready for more Vancouver Dominators

Preorder
Two Minutes for Holding
Coming March 2025

https://geni.us/TwoMinutesforHolding

Playing the Neutral Zone
Coming June 2025

https://geni.us/PlayingtheNeutralZone

Through the Five Hole
Coming September 2025

Ready for More Vancouver Dominators

https://geni.us/ThroughtheFiveHole

Get a Free Book

GET A FREE BOOK

Sign up for my newsletter and I'll send you a free book.

https://geni.us/NLSignupBackMatter

Follow S.L. Sterling

Follow S.L. Sterling

Did you know that bookbub has a feature where you can follow me and it will send you an alert when I release a book or put a title on sale? Sign up here and make sure you stay in the loop.

Bookbub:
https://geni.us/SLSterlingBookbub

Website
https://www.authorslsterling.com

Facebook
https://geni.us/SLSterlingFB

Twitter
https://geni.us/SLSterlingTwitter

Instagram
https://geni.us/SLSterlingInstagram

Tiktok
https://geni.us/slsterlingtiktok

Reader Group
https://geni.us/SapphiresReaderGroup

Goodreads
https://geni.us/SterlingGoodreads

Newsletter
https://geni.us/NLSignupBackMatter

USA Today Bestselling Author S.L. Sterling was born and raised in southern Ontario. She is married to her best friend and soul mate and lives in Northern Ontario Canada. They have two Alaskan Malamutes.

An avid reader all her life, S.L. Sterling dreamt of becoming an author. She decided to give writing a try after one of her favorite authors launched a course on how to write your novel. This course gave her the push she needed to put pen to paper and her debut novel "It Was Always You" was born.

When S.L. Sterling isn't writing or plotting her next novel she can be found curled up with a cup of coffee, blanket and the newest romance novel from one of her favorite authors.

In her spare time, she enjoys camping, hiking, sunny destinations, spending quality time with family and friends and of course reading.

To be notified of new releases or sales, join S.L.
Sterling's private Mailing List.
https://geni.us/NLSignupBackMatter

Get even more of the inside scoop when you join S.L.
Sterling's private Facebook group, Sterling's Silver
Sapphires: https://geni.us/SapphiresReaderGroup

Other Books by S.L. Sterling

It Was Always You

On A Silent Night

Bad Company

Back to You this Christmas

Fireside Love

Holiday Wishes

Saviour Boy

The Boy Under the Gazebo

The Greatest Gift

Into the Sunset

Letting You Go

Spencer Brooks Diaries

Our Little Secret

Our Little Surprise

Our Little Wedding

The Malone Brother Series

A Kiss Beneath the Stars

In Your Arms

His to Hold

Finding Forever with You

Vegas MMA

Dagger

Doctors of Eastport General

Doctor Desire

Doctor Right

Doctor Frost

All I Want for Christmas (Contemporary Romance Holiday
Collection)

Willow Valley

Memories of the Past

To Trust my Heart (The Holiday Dilemma)

Letters from the Heart

What Once was Broken (My Darling Christmas)

Scars on my Heart

The Happy Holidates Series

Pop Tarts and Mistletoe

Champagne and Fireworks

Summer Nights and Fireflies

Vancouver Dominators

Inside the Penalty Box

Ten Minute Misconduct

Crossing the Red Line